Sugar Creek Inn

A New England Novel

Sharon Snow Sirois

LIGHTHOUSE PUBLISHING

North Haven, Connecticut

D1057549

LIGHTHOUSE PUBLISHING
P.O. Box 396
North Haven, CT 06473

Illustration by Beverly Rich
Computer Graphics by Jane Lyman

Library of Congress Control Number 2002103429

International Standard Book Number 0-9679052-8-1

Printed in the United States of America

I would like to thank God for allowing me to use my gift to bring glory to Him. I am completely overwhelmed, humbled and awed by our God. He gives me the inspiration to write stories about New England, which is an area that I love so much. The closer I grow to God, the more clearly I see that He truly is the very life inside of me.

"For I know the plans I have for you," declares the Lord, "plans to prosper you and not harm you, plans to give you hope and a future. Then you will call upon me, and come and pray to me, and I will listen to you. You will seek me, and find me when you seek me with all your heart."

JEREMIAH 29: 11-13

To the Readers

Dear Friends,

I wanted to thank you so much for all your letters, cards, and emails. Your support has encouraged me as well as my entire family. Your prayers are something that I value more then words can say! Thank you!

Many of you have asked me where I get my ideas. I have lived in New England all my life, and my mind just naturally cranks out stories from the places that I've been. *Sawyer's Crossing*, the first book in the New England Novel series, is set in Vermont. I spent a lot of time in Vermont as a kid because that's where my dad grew up, and we have relatives there. I have always loved covered bridges and enjoyed growing up around them. They became the personal forts for my brother, sister and me. We spent hours climbing the trusses of the bridge and dangling from the rafters like a bunch of monkeys. A good bridge always had a rope underneath it. There is nothing like swinging on a rope across river rapids to fill a kid's imagination with stories. I've always loved adventure. I knew that I would write a police novel someday, because my brother, whom I've always adored, became a police officer. I listened to his stories with great interest and loved when I got to ride around with him in his squad car. Parts of *Sawyer's Crossing* definitely came from those times.

Sugar Creek Inn is set on beautiful Eagle Lake in Maine. Some of the background for this book came from working as a camp counselor, and the summer my sister and I spent working at a Christian inn on Lake Sunapee, in New Hampshire. We were cooks, waitresses, chambermaids, and your basic summer slaves! I learned the correct way to make a bed, and the quickest way to short sheet one! (This is living proof that the skills you learn as a child will be used in your adult life! Again, and again...) I also learned to carry a loaded tray without dumping it over on any the customers. (This is a skill that should never be taken for granted...trust me on this!) It was during that summer that I learned to make my first police car. (This is a scoop of vanilla ice cream, a dab of chocolate sauce, and a bright red cherry on top.)

On our time off, we got to enjoy the waterfront. Swimming, water skiing, and sailing were great perks of being on staff. I loved sailing out to the islands to explore. Working at the inn that summer left me with wonderful memories. I loved working on staff, and I enjoyed meeting the guests.

Thank you again for your prayers and letters. I am humbled that you've allowed me to become a part of your life. You've become a very special part of mine!

God Bless,
Sharon Snow Sirois

I love to hear from my readers!
You can write me through Lighthouse Publishing, P.O. Box 396, North Haven, CT 06473 or email me at sharonsnowsirois@hotmail.com

Acknowledgments

I'd like to thank the people at Lighthouse Publishing. A strong dedicated team working behind the scenes is how a dream becomes a reality. Your wisdom, insight, and advice never cease to amaze me. You do an excellent job bringing the book through its many stages. Thank you for all your long hours on this project. Thank you for your prayers, support, and encouragement.

Karol Ann Shalvoy. Thank you for the excellent job you do editing the stories that bounce around in my head. Your long hours, insightful direction, and dedication help make this book the best it can be. You are one of the most giving people I have ever met. Thank you for your prayers, support, encouragement, friendship, and the daily supply of coffee and junk food you send my way.

Beverly Rich. You never cease to amaze me with your artistic abilities. Thanks for the wonderful job you did on *Sugar Creek Inn*. The illustration is exactly what I had in my mind.

Richard Shalvoy. Hey, why approach my computer problems rationally and calmly when I can go straight to all out panic! Thanks for all the times you've bailed me out of computer jams. Your expertise in this area is greatly appreciated.

Patricia Stearns. Thank you for the excellent work you did proofing the manuscript. You are so great at catching all those little things that I don't even see! Thanks for your encouragement and support.

Jane Lyman. Thank you for the wonderful job you did with the computer graphics. Your commitment to excellence helps make this book the best it can be.

Margaret George. You are the most amazing Bible resource person that I know. You're always able to find the verses that I'm hunting for, unless it's one of those times my mind has combined verses and hymns to come up with its own unique combination! Thanks for your patience and help.

The Snow & Sirois Families. Thank you for all your prayers, support and encouragement. I really treasure the times we get to spend together. You are all so special to me. I love you with all my heart!

Peter. There are simply no words to describe how deeply you have touched my life. You are a wonderful husband, father, and best friend. You inspire me, encourage me, and support me. You are always there for me, and believe in me, and this means more to me then you'll ever know. Thank you for your strong commitment to God and your family. You are such a special person. I love you and cherish you.

Jennifer, John, Robert, Michael. You are a gift that I treasure with all my heart. I am so proud of you guys. You are so special. I love being your mom.

This one is for my kids
Jennifer, John, Robert, Michael

One of the earliest memories I have from childhood is wanting to be a mom. When my first grade teacher had the class choose a career, I remember writing down "mom." I'll never forget the teacher calling me to her desk and telling me I couldn't be a mom for a career. I burst out crying, and she quickly changed her mind! I can't tell you how excited I was when each one of you was born! You guys are sensitive, smart, and very funny. Our home rings out with laughter a lot! I am in awe as I watch God working in your lives. You totally amaze me with your spiritual insights. I love the verses that you leave on my desk to encourage me. You are definitely learning what the joy of giving is all about. Your kind and generous spirit has reached out in so many ways. I am so proud of your work with Operation Shoebox. You save your allowance and collect items year around to fill shoeboxes for the homeless shelters. You're making a difference in your corner of the world.

As you go through life and all the uncertainties it can bring, here are some things that I can tell you for sure that will never change. Dad and I will always be there for you and love you with all our hearts. God loves us more then we can ever imagine. God is faithful, unbelievably good, and He is always with us. God will always do what He has said He will do. You can trust Him with your life, because His promises are true. I have learned that we don't need to follow God full of confidence and courage. He takes us where we are. Remember-being in the minority is not wrong; it's just usually less crowded. The important thing is that you follow God no matter what. Don't look at this world through your eyes, look at it through the heart that God has given you. It doesn't matter if we can't see the end of the road or understand how things are going to work out. We have a Heavenly Father that approaches life in a heavenly way. As we start to walk in His ways, even on shaky legs, He will give us strength, courage, confidence, and peace to meet each challenge. Don't hesitate to follow God in what He is calling you to do.

At times our mind limits God because we cannot comprehend how He can do what He says He will do. Miracles come in all shapes and sizes. The Bible is proof of God's excellent track record. He defeated the enemies, knocked down the walls of Jericho, parted the Red Sea, used a boy to kill a giant with a single stone, and raised Jesus from the dead. There are so many more. Never once did God go back on His word or break a single promise. Follow Him with all your heart, one step at a time. Be prepared to be amazed, awed, blown away, and completely humbled. He is a totally awesome God, and all you'll ever need.

I am honored and blessed to be your mom. You are a gift that I treasure with all my heart.

I love you !
mom ☺

*"Be strong and courageous. Do not be afraid;
do not be discouraged,
for the Lord your God is with you
wherever you go."*

JOSHUA 1:9

One

$\mathcal{M}$atthew stared out his front window in total disbelief at the procession parading up his front brick walk. There were three women purposefully marching toward his little Cape Cod house with such determination that he felt as though his fortress were under attack. His first instinct was to pull the shades down and run for the basement. Taking cover did not seem like an option here. It seemed like a matter of survival.

Yet as he quickly started to turn away from the window, one of the attackers spied him and eagerly waved. He cringed inside, realizing he had been spotted. He would boldly have to face this convoy head-on.

A moment later, enthusiastic pounding on the front door told him that the circus had arrived. As he cautiously opened his front door, the group pushed past him and immediately invaded the inside of the little house. He watched, torn between confusion and amusement, as the three women loudly went in the general direction of the kitchen.

The spectacle they created was a momentary diversion away from their initial attack.

"Here we are!" the oldest girl announced, confidently and enthusiastically, as though he had been waiting all his life to see them. To say that his current situation was bizarre would seem like a severe understatement. "I've baked my famous chicken casserole, which I'm going to pop into your oven now."

She stated this information proudly, as she marched past the bewildered man. She failed to notice that he was still holding the doorknob tightly enough to turn his knuckles white. The gang of girls made its way through his small living room and into his even smaller kitchen.

"And," the oldest girl continued on easily, as though she were talking to a lifelong friend, "here's my delicious chocolate cake. It's to die for. I baked it just this afternoon. You're going to love it…everyone does! But," she said, waving a finger at him teasingly, "don't ask me for the recipe. It's an old family secret. It's been in the Miller family for over a hundred years…"

Before she could rattle on, the perplexed young man blurted out in a voice that was filled with relief, "Oh, you're the Millers!"

All three girls stopped the tasks they were doing, and in complete sync, turned and stared at the young man. For the first time they noticed that he hadn't moved from the spot where he had opened the door.

"Of course we're the Millers," the middle girl stated, as though to consider anything else would be completely ridiculous.

She was very athletic looking, and she held an edge of toughness that the other two did not possess. Some little voice inside of him warned him to tread carefully where this feisty girl was concerned.

"Who else would we be?" she asked, appraising him suspiciously. "Didn't the Hobson brothers tell you we were coming over?"

"You are the new Pastor at Eagle Lake Bible Chapel, aren't you?" The youngest girl spoke quietly, with an expression on her face that was an interesting mixture of panic and shyness. "You are Matthew Bishop, aren't you?" she asked leaning toward him slightly.

This snapped Matthew out of his trance. "Yes. Yes, I am," he stuttered in an awkward response.

"I apologize for taking you by surprise," the oldest girl responded sincerely. "We thought the Hobson brothers told you we were coming."

Matthew relaxed enough to finally release the doorknob. He was vaguely aware of his aching hand. "Yes." A touch of amusement brushed his face. "The Hobson brothers told me that the Miller's were coming over to help me move in, but I distinctly remember them saying Max Miller's boys."

As soon as the words were out of his mouth, Matthew knew something funny was up. Wide, audacious smiles swept across the three ladies' faces, and it appeared to him that they were trying hard to hold back their laughter. They weren't successful for long, and soon it bubbled freely throughout the small cape. The sound of the laughter was like music to Matthew's ears. It warmed his homesick heart, if only for a second, and he was grateful for the moment. Yet, at the same time, he had a strong suspicion that he was the butt of their joke. Until he found out exactly what was so comical, he was determined to keep his expression quite serious.

As the girls came toward him, with their hands extended welcomingly, Matthew immediately noticed two things. First was the strong family resemblance among the girls. They all had big, brown eyes and straight, light brown hair. The two older girls wore their hair very short, yet the younger girl had hair that went halfway down her back. The other thing that Matthew noticed was how tall the girls were. They each towered over him by several inches. He knew most people did. An adult man of twenty-eight standing only 5'5" had most junior high kids towering over him.

Matthew shook the first hand that reached him. It belonged to the oldest girl. Her voice was friendly and light. "Hi, I'm Andy Miller Wallace, and I'm so sorry that we startled you. I'm the oldest Miller daughter. I'm married to Ethan Wallace, and I have a two-year-old son, Nicholas." Andy paused, and turned slightly toward the other two girls in the room. "These are my two sisters, Jay and Sam."

"How many girls are in your family?" Matthew asked inquiringly. The girls laughed kindly, and Matthew knew that he had just made his first real friends at Sugar Creek. They were caring and sincere, and on top of it all, very funny.

"My parents had four girls in six years! Can you believe it!" Andy spoke in an animated fashion, with her arms waving around. "Jack's the youngest. She's twenty-two. She wanted to be here, too, but she had to pick up her fiancé from the airport."

"Four girls in one family!" The new pastor shook his head in awe. "You could probably write a book on sibling relationships."

The girls laughed. Suddenly Jay became serious. "There are many ingredients that make up a true sibling relationship. Sympathy, I've found from experience, is oftentimes not one of them." Everyone laughed.

"Sisters...," Andy tried to sound menacing. "You can't live with them, and you can't kill them!" Everyone laughed again.

"Your brothers probably don't stand a chance at getting into the bathroom in the morning," Matthew laughed as he tried to envision four girls, all around the same age, under one roof.

"And that is probably why God didn't give us any brothers," Jay said defensively. "They wouldn't have been able to handle us!"

Matthew's face scrunched up, and he gave the girls a look that was nothing short of total confusion. "Roy and Ray Hobson said Max Miller had boys."

The girls laughed so hard, they almost laughed Matthew right out of his own house. "You see," Sam began softly, "my father wanted four boys, and God gave him four girls! So, he gave us all boys' names!" The girls laughed again, good-naturedly. "Everyone on the lake refers to us as Max Miller's boys."

The shocked expression on Matthew's face made the girls laugh all over again. "What are your names again?" he asked inquisitively, taking a step closer to them.

"I'm Andy," the oldest girl identified herself quickly. "My legal name is Andrea, but everyone calls me Andy."

"I'm Jayme," the middle one stated firmly. "I've never been called by that, so don't start. Everyone calls me Jay."

"OK, I'll do that," Matthew smiled, grateful for the warning.

"I'm Samantha," the shy girl said softly. "I've always been called Sam."

Matthew nodded at her, and then said, "How about the youngest one. What was her name again?"

"Oh, that's Jack," Andy quickly volunteered. "Her legal name is Jacilyn."

"Yeah, and no one but Bradley calls her that," Jay said sourly.

"Who's Bradley?" Matthew asked, trying to place this Sugar Creek crew.

"Someone you'd rather not know," Jay added sarcastically.

"Jay, that's not nice," Sam reprimanded her quickly.

"It may not be nice, but it's true." Jay was clearly challenging Sam to deny it.

"Bradley is Jack's fiancé." Andy was diplomatic in her approach. "Jack has known Bradley since she was eight."

"Really?" Matthew asked interestedly.

"Yes," Andy said, going back to the stove to check on her casserole. "I suspect theirs is the first wedding you'll be performing in Sugar Creek."

"When are they getting married?" Matthew asked curiously.

"Beginning of September." Jay's tone was dismal.

Matthew couldn't help but notice the grim expressions that fell across the sisters' faces. "And why do I get the feeling that this isn't good?"

Andy instinctively slid a hand over Jay's mouth. "Let him judge the situation for himself," she was firm with her sister. "He will meet both of them tomorrow."

Jay growled under her breath, but didn't say a word.

"Oh, I almost forgot," Andy slapped the side of her head. "My parents would love to have you over to the Inn for lunch after the service tomorrow."

"Oh, that's right," Matthew nodded his head. "Your family runs the Sugar Creek Inn."

"Yes," Sam spoke in her usual quiet manner. "It's about halfway down the lake from here, on the same side."

"Well, please tell your parents that I'd be happy to come for lunch tomorrow."

"You might not be saying that after you sit through a meal with Bradley," Jay added quickly. "We call him Mr. Indigestion…"

"Jay," Andy's voice was growing angry. She grabbed her sister's arm and shoved her out the door, "I'm warning you!"

"Yeah, well, I'm warning him," Jay grumbled loudly. "It's only fair."

"He's really not that bad," Sam said. Matthew smiled at her. She was definitely the peacemaker between her sisters.

"He's worse!" Jay said as Andy dragged her down the steps.

"Come on, Sunshine," Andy teased her middle sister, "we've got housework to do."

"I read an article last week that said if you do housework right, it could kill you!" Jay's expression was completely serious as she glanced back toward Matthew.

"Then you'd better be careful," Matthew grinned at her.

"Will you come on, Jay!" Andy was growing frustrated.

"Remember what I said about sympathy?" Jay shouted to Matthew.

Matthew just nodded and laughed. The Miller girls were the funniest people he'd met in a long time.

"If you don't get in this truck, Jay, I may have to kill you," Andy joked as she shoved Jay toward the old blue Chevy.

"I thought you said before that you couldn't ever kill your own sister!" Jay said, proudly quoting Andy's line back to her.

"Yeah, well, you'd better watch out. I think I may be changing my mind about that!" Andy's tone was spunky.

As Andy shoved Jay toward an old, blue pickup truck, she suddenly stopped.

"Pastor," Andy's words came out in a rush, "welcome to Sugar Creek. It was nice meeting you."

The girls waved good-bye again and piled into the old truck. As Matthew watched his new friends disappear down the road, he felt a sense of excitement, mixed with a generous dose of dread, for the day that was to come. His gut feelings were usually remarkably right. And this time, his gut feelings told him he was not only heading for trouble, but heading for it at two hundred miles an hour.

Two

 $\mathcal{J}$ ack sat with her sisters—second pew from the front—in the quaint, white, wood-paneled, traditional New-England-style church. With only sixteen pews in the entire sanctuary, Eagle Lake Bible Chapel wasn't considered large by any means. Just the same, Jack eagerly kept an eye out for a glimpse of the new pastor, as though she thought she might miss him. A new pastor was big news in a small town like Sugar Creek. As Jack looked around her, not only could she feel the anticipation mounting, she could tell most everyone had their eyes peeled for the grand entrance.

"I can't believe you guys won't tell me what he looks like," Jack complained quietly, as she fidgeted restlessly in the hard wooden pew. "You are so mean."

"We don't want to get you upset," Jay's tone was matter of fact, as she casually glanced out the twelve-pane window she sat next to. "He kind of has the type of face that would be good for radio."

Jack's brown eyebrows shot up. "You're just saying that to get me upset," she whispered angrily. "You know I don't want anyone from the Munsters or Addams Family marrying me."

"Maybe you should have a radio service," Jay offered helpfully. "That could actually work well all the way around. No one would notice the new pastor's mug, and you wouldn't have to worry about spending a lot on your wedding outfits." Jay smiled at Jack enthusiastically. "This is going to be great! Leave the details to me."

"Go away…"Jack's voice was so low that it actually sounded like a growl. "I may kick you out of the wedding party."

"Don't do me any favors!" Jay shot back sarcastically, as she absent-mindedly dug the toe of her black shoe into the sanctuary's old maroon carpeting. "Besides," she rolled her eyes at her engaged sister, "Mom would never let you. She's determined to see me dressed up in some flowery, ruffled, feminine-type getup. This whole thing is completely ridiculous, if you ask me."

"I wasn't asking you," Jack said in a tight voice, staring hard at her sister.

"I thought you'd want to know anyways…,"Jay stated in an insulted tone, as she shrugged her shoulders indifferently.

"You were wrong," Jack said flatly.

"I know this may be hard to believe," Jay said evenly, "but, once in a while I am."

"Will you two stop it?" Andy felt completely annoyed. "You're acting like you're two-year-olds."

Jay stopped talking, but sat stiffly in the uncomfortable, mahogany pew. She started humming the theme song to the Munsters, just loud enough for Jack to hear it. Jack glared at her through hot, squinted eyes.

"Andy, you've got to help me out here. Please," Jack begged, in a distressed voice, "tell me if he's really as bad as Jay is saying. I've got to know."

"No one," Andy's tone was confident, "is ever as bad as Jay says."

"That's true!" Relief instantly washed over her. "That is definitely true."

"He sort of looks similar to old Pastor Clayton." Andy scrunched her brow thoughtfully.

"What do you mean by 'sort of'?" Jack asked her oldest sister in an investigative tone. "That phrase worries me. It implies far too much."

"Well," Andy started to play with the hem on her spring floral dress, "what's to say? He's old, bald, and has huge bushy eyebrows on him, like he's got hedges glued to the front of his forehead."

"And," Jay leaned toward her sister, "a pot on the front of him that would make an old, muddy pig proud."

"No way!" Jack was completely horrified. "And this is the man who's going to marry Bradley and me."

"Maybe it's not too late for you to join the Methodist Church on the other side of the lake," Jay said brightly. "Their pastor's old, but has taken care of himself well. And, since Bradley goes there, I bet they'd zip your membership right through."

Sam shook her head at her sisters disapprovingly. "You are simply awful. We're talking about a man of God here. Have some respect." Her sisters completely ignored her.

"Maybe Dad can convince Pastor Clayton to come back and marry me," Jack's voice held a note a hope. "After all, he is the pastor that I grew up with." Jack was so absorbed in her thoughts that she didn't notice the smiles spreading on her sisters' faces.

A moment later, Jack turned to the sister on her right. Sam was sixteen months older than Jack, yet the two of them were closer than two peas in a pod. "Sam," she whispered quietly, "what do you think about the new pastor?'

Sam smiled slowly and kindly. It was a smile that Jack had always loved. It was warm and sincere, like the person who gave it, and above all, it was honest. Jack knew she could always depend on Sam for an honest opinion.

"Well, it's not as bad as they say," Sam commented thoughtfully.

"Yeah, but it's not as good as I'm hoping for either, is it?" Jack demanded, struggling to keep her voice quiet. "This is just not going to be good. I know it."

"You're going to like him, Jack," Sam was quick to reassure her. "He's very kind."

"Yeah, but Jay says he's got a face made for radio," Jack couldn't help but struggle with the thought.

"You don't have to feature him in your wedding album, Jack," Sam teased. "Besides, you know you shouldn't judge a book by its cover. God wants us to look on the heart of a person. And," Sam said, smiling sweetly, "if you get past the cover, you will find Pastor Bishop to be a very nice man."

"Nice man…" Jack repeated to herself uneasily. "I'm not sure that's the quality I'm going for here…"

"Well, you should be, Jack," Sam scolded her younger sister. "You really should know better."

A moment later, her father was leading the church in the opening hymn. Max Miller was a tall, thin man in his early fifties, with very little brown hair left on his balding head. He wore round, preppy-style glasses, and a smile that would make anyone feel downright welcome. He was an easygoing man with a kind, gentle spirit. Max had a way of energizing the congregation, and getting them to focus their hearts on the Lord. As the voices rose in song, Jack forced her mind away from the new-pastor issue and focused on the hymn she was singing. How Great Thou Art had been a favorite since childhood. God's greatness did nothing short of completely amazing her. When she put her thoughts on the Lord and dwelt on His power and greatness, she was simply brought to a place of awe. It was a place of humbleness and respect. It was a place where no mere words could describe her feelings.

As the hymn ended, her father went to the podium and began a lengthy introduction of the new pastor. As Jack stared at the podium, for the first time she noticed a shiny black shoe. It belonged to someone who was hidden behind the podium. Jack turned and glanced at Andy for any clues, yet the eldest Miller girl just stared straight ahead. Whoever this man was, Jack thought curiously, he was so short that the podium was literally blocking him.

As her father finally introduced Pastor Matthew Bishop and he stood up and came forward, Jack's mouth dropped open so far that it almost hit the floor. She quickly put a hand over the gaping hole, yet not before the young man at the podium noticed it. He paused, looked momentarily at her, and then directed his attention to his new congregation and addressed them.

Jack kept her eyes glued to her hands in her lap. She knew from the heat that she felt on her cheeks that her face must have looked red enough to explode. And to make matters worse, she could hear the quiet yet steady laughter that her sisters were working hard to try to muffle. They had pulled a good one over on her, and they knew it. She would think of ways later to repay their kindness.

Matthew Bishop was not a balding, heavy, old man. He was, in fact, a gorgeous-looking young man, with the most attractive, stunning smile that Jack had ever seen. And he was probably only a few years older than herself.

As Jack buried her embarrassment, she took a chance and slowly glanced up. Pastor Bishop stood in front of the podium, not behind it, and was talking with ease to the people. His voice was gentle and kind, and his expressive brown eyes were filled with tenderness and care. Jack couldn't tear herself away from those gentle brown eyes. They reeled her in, like a fish on a line. She found them intriguing, and yet at the same time flooding over with a depth of love and compassion that she had never seen before. They stirred her to her very soul. As she continued to stare at his eyes, she soon found herself under his direct gaze. He was still preaching, and it panicked Jack a bit to think that she couldn't recall a word of his sermon. The only thing that she could recall was the fact that this young, extremely good-looking pastor had incredible, luring brown eyes.

Once again, Jack's eyes retreated to her lap. She knew that he knew she had been staring at him. Embarrassment flooded her face for the second time that morning. Jack shook her head slowly. What in the world was wrong with her? She was never one to gawk or stare at men, not to even mention that she was an engaged woman. Yet, for some reason, this man standing before her was a man she was finding it very difficult to take her eyes off of. It was very much out of character for her.

As she slowly lifted her eyes from the safety of her lap and back to the preacher, her heart stopped beating. He was looking at her, so directly in fact, it was as if he were simply waiting for her to bring her eyes back up to meet his. When she did, he held her eyes with his own, just long enough for her to know that he was on to her game. A brief smile touched his lips, and he raised his eyebrows slightly, almost challengingly. Then, with full attention, he directed his energy back to his sermon.

Once again, Jack directed her attention back to her lap. This time, however, her sisters did the same. All four of them were studying their laps as intently as if the secrets of the universe had just fallen into them.

A firm, yet quiet, clearing of the throat made all the girls look across the aisle. The stern expression on their father's face told them all they needed to know. He had observed the whole charade, and basically they would be grounded for life once the sermon was over. They were familiar with the expression. Unfortunately, it had been one they had seen too often growing up.

As the service ended, the new pastor went to the back of the congregation to greet his new flock. The four sisters rapidly went in the opposite direction. "We've already met him," Andy teased Jack softly. "Are you sure you don't want to say hi?"

"I'm not speaking to any of you right now," Jack hissed angrily at them. "And for the record, I may never speak to any of you again!"

"Is that a promise?" Jay asked hopefully.

Jack glared at her sister.

"Pastor was right," Jay went on obnoxiously. "Good things happen to those that wait on the Lord. By the way," Jay gently touched Jack's shoulder, "that was the main point of the sermon today, in case you hadn't noticed." She wiggled her eyebrows at Jack. "You did seem a little preoccupied."

"You're cruel!" Jack said through clenched teeth.

"That's nothing new to you." Jay's tone was void of any sympathy in the slightest. "Besides, I did owe you big time."

"What did I ever do to you?" Jack asked innocently.

Jay eyed her younger sister evenly. "I could write a book."

"I meant recently," Jack added quickly.

"Did you say recently?" Jay asked challengingly. "Well, I'll tell you recently. Remember last week when Nicholas stuck a sticker of Barney the purple dinosaur to my butt, and you never told me? Remember that? I walked all over town that day with Barney stuck on my rear, and no one told me. You saw him do it, and you never said a thing."

Jack's smirk turned into loud laughter. "I meant to tell you. It's just that as you were going out the door, new guests arrived at the Inn. I was busy checking them in."

"You couldn't have taken a second to tell me, Jack?" Jay said angrily. "Do you have any idea how embarrassing it is to walk around town with Barney stuck on your backside. I should think of something especially mean to do to you for that one alone."

"OK, you two," Andy stepped in as referee. "Back to your corners, now. Besides," she couldn't help but laugh at the story, "Nicholas is two. You wouldn't believe half of the things he's done to Ethan alone. You should always be careful around two-year-olds."

"Dad's going to kill us for fooling around in church." Sam's voice was filled with regret. "I had wanted to sail over to Blueberry Island this afternoon. Now, I bet we'll be grounded for the day, with a long list of chores to do."

"It was worth it," Andy laughed loudly. "Did you see Jack's face? It was worth every minute."

"It's not fair. Dad won't ground you anymore because you're married." Jack paused and looked at her older sister seriously. In a scolding tone, she stated evenly, "You're supposed to be mature, you know. You really should know better than this."

Andy laughed loudly again. "I know. But somehow, hanging around with the three of you makes me regress. My maturity level drops drastically. Don't worry, I'll hang around and help you with whatever punishment Dad levels on you."

"That's fair of you," Sam nodded thoughtfully.

"She's just saying that because Nicholas has an awful cold, and she doesn't want to be around a grumpy tot," Jay muttered accusingly.

"That's not true," Andy was clearly insulted. "Don't make me take back my offer."

"Sorry," Jay grumbled.

"You should be," Andy glared at her for a second. "Now, let's go and face the music. And, by the way, Jack," Andy turned to her youngest sister, "I think I forgot to mention that Pastor Bishop is coming for lunch."

Jack groaned loudly, and the older sisters just laughed all over again. This day had gone from bad to worse. "Just let me live through it, God," Jack prayed sincerely. "And if You want to rapture me now...it's a good time."

Three

Jack couldn't believe her bad luck. Her father had seated her directly across the table from Matthew Bishop. There was no place to run and hide from him now. Even when she wasn't trying to look at him, she felt as though it appeared she was looking at him. And the more she honestly tried not to look in his direction, the more she caught herself doing just that.

Jack purposely made herself focus in on the others around the large, rectangular, mahogany table. All her family was there, including Ethan, Andy's husband, and their two-year-old son Nicholas. At the far end of the antique table were Roy and Ray Hobson. They were retired brothers in their eighties who had been permanent guests at the Inn since Jack was five. They were like doting grandfathers to her.

Yet even with all the others around the table, Jack found it increasingly uncomfortable to be seated across the table from Matthew Bishop. His unobstructed, direct line of vision of her was completely unnerving her. Every time they made eye contact, it was as though Matthew held her captive with those tender brown eyes of his. The silent communication was louder than any words. Something was happening between their hearts, and it frightened Jack beyond her imagination.

Right after her father had said the blessing and they began to pass the food around the table, Bradley finally made his entrance. Jack couldn't hide her smile as he walked into the room. Bradley Clarke, at 6'4", with broad shoulders and shining blue eyes, looked like the poster boy for what the perfect image of an all-American-boy should be. Not only was he good looking, but he seemed to carry himself with a sense of regal confidence. The fact that Bradley had given his heart to Christ at a young age and desired to serve Him from the pulpit as a preacher only made Jack admire him more.

Bradley immediately introduced himself to Matthew Bishop. "Pastor Bishop," he said very self-assuredly, "welcome to Sugar Creek."

"Thank you, Bradley," Matthew answered sincerely. "You're home from college on spring break, I understand."

Bradley nodded, while he stuffed his mouth full of buttery mashed potato.

"What are you studying?" Matthew inquired.

A wide, certain smile crossed Bradley's face. "Why, I'm studying to be a pastor, like you," he stated proudly. "I'll graduate from seminary in August, and then Jacilyn and I will be married in early September."

Smiles spread around the room as the engaged couple talked a little about the upcoming wedding. Yet, Matthew couldn't help but notice the forced, almost painful smile that Jack had plastered across her face. Most brides-to-be he knew were bubbling over with excitement and joy. This was definitely not the case here, and he intended to find out why before he was supposed to marry the couple.

As Bradley continued to discuss the wedding plans, Jack grew unusually quiet. Every time he referred to her as Jacilyn, she cringed inside a little. Ever since they were kids he had called her by her formal name. He said Jack was a boy's name, and he refused to call his beautiful girl by a rugged-sounding boy's name. It had always annoyed her. But now, for some reason, it annoyed her even more. Jack was her name. She felt comfortable with it. She was such a tomboy that it seemed to fit her better than a formal-sounding name like Jacilyn.

"That's a serious face," Matthew commented quietly, leaning towards Jack slightly.

Jack smiled at him awkwardly, and then looked away. There was something distinctly unsettling about the pastor's gaze. It was almost as if his compassionate eyes could read her mind. Jack knew she had the unfortunate habit of wearing her emotions on her face. She had since childhood. All her thoughts...the good, the bad, and the ugly...paraded across her face for all the world to see. The only way she could combat the situation was to avoid direct eye contact with people. And right now, Matthew Bishop's tender gaze was something she desperately wanted to avoid. He saw too much. She hid too little. It was a revealing situation that she didn't want revealed.

As casually as she could, Jack replied in a dismissive tone, "Oh, I was just thinking."

"A penny for your thoughts?" Matthew asked curiously, smiling kindly at her.

Jack had to laugh. For as much as she wanted to avoid this man, at the same time, she felt drawn to him in a way that she had never been drawn to anyone in her life. She laughed again, and then said in a teasing tone, "Pastor Bishop, you are a total cheapskate!"

Matthew's jaw dropped slightly, and he appeared completely stunned. Jack watched in amusement as his eyebrows rose in a clueless configuration. The man was clearly taken off guard.

Jack laughed again, and then said in a joking tone, "You see, with inflation and all, I figure my thoughts should be worth a quarter...at the very least."

Matthew smiled at her and laughed softly. "That sounds like a fair minimum." They held each other's eyes for a moment, and in that instant, Jack couldn't turn away. She couldn't breathe, move, or think. A feeling washed over her that she had never experienced before. She fought quickly to classify it, but came up empty. The connection between them was so strong, and so electric, that the house could have been on fire, and still Jack would have been unable to move.

Bradley cleared his throat loudly, and then said in a smug tone, "That's my girl." He possessively positioned his arm around Jack's shoulders, and drew her toward him in an uncomfortable embrace. "She's always thinking. Jacilyn's the brains out of the two of us." He stared at Matthew closely. "God knew what He was doing when He put the two of us together."

Jack forced a smile at the compliment. She felt embarrassed beyond words. Here she was, with her fiancé, at her family's dinner table, gawking at the new pastor. She was completely unable to take her eyes off the man. Awkwardness flooded her. Jack didn't understand, for the life of her, why she couldn't get a grip on the situation. If she could only understand what the situation was, she knew that would help. What in the world was happening between her and Matthew Bishop. Whatever it was, she thought tensely, it had better stop now. She just wished she understood whatever it was, because it would make it a whole lot easier to stop. For the second time in one day, the whole rapture idea seemed very appealing.

Bradley squeezed her hand and brought her mind back to reality. "I'd like to go for a walk with you before I leave for school." His tone was entirely too serious for Jack. She knew he wanted answers about her unexpected behavior. Yet, Jack thought nervously, how could she give him answers to something she didn't understand herself?

"I'm afraid Jack and her sisters will be doing a long list of chores this afternoon." Maxwell Miller's tone was firm and unyielding.

Jack silently thanked her father, while her sisters just groaned. She had never been so glad, or so relieved, to receive a punishment in her life. Pile them on, she thought eagerly. She found herself actually looking forward to her chores. It would kill two birds with one stone. It would get her away from Bradley and Matthew, which in her opinion couldn't happen fast enough. It would also ensure her the privacy she desperately needed to think about those same two men. She felt confident that with some serious thought she could work this situation out.

"Were you girls fooling around in church again?" Bradley demanded. The disgust in his voice was clearly evident. The silence he received from the girls was all the confirmation he needed.

Jack earnestly prayed that this can of worms would not be opened up right now. She had no excuse for her odd behavior. She knew, without a doubt, there was no way she would come out looking good here. Not in the very least. The situation was entirely unredeemable. She shut her eyes for a moment hoping for the best, yet anticipating the worst.

"Jacilyn," Bradley scolded, "you're going to be a pastor's wife. This really has to stop." Quiet laughter rumbled around the table, as all eyes watched the young, engaged couple.

She quickly agreed with Bradley. It did have to stop. Yet how she was going to go about stopping the entire situation still remained a deep mystery. She anxiously tried to formulate a plan in her mind. Plan A. Plan B. It didn't matter right now as long as she had some sort of a plan. A plan meant hope. It would be something she could grab onto and put into action. Unfortunately, she couldn't come up with any instant, miraculous plan, and that left the hopeless situation even bleaker.

"Pastor Bishop," Ray Hobson spoke up from his spot at the far end of the table, "I enjoyed your sermon today."

"I especially enjoyed the sideshow," his brother Roy whispered in a voice just loud enough to be heard. Laughter broke out all around the table.

"Sideshow?" Bradley stated in an alarmed tone. "What exactly did go on this morning?"

"I'd like to know myself," Roy grinned broadly at the sisters. "From where I sat, I could see just enough to know that I was missing something interesting." Everyone roared with laughter again.

Once the laughter died down, Andy diplomatically answered, "Oh, it was really nothing at all."

"From where Roy and I were sitting," Ray pointed out humorously, "I'd have to say that there was a whole lot of nothing going on." The Hobson brothers, at ages eighty-three and eighty- five, could hold their own, in a comical sense, better than anyone Jack knew. Not much ever slipped past their hawk-eyes or radar-like ears. They were truly remarkable.

Laughter erupted around the table, as the eyes focused on the sisters for any clues they might give up. They remained tight-lipped.

"We're going to have to talk about this eventually, Girls," Max said good-naturedly.

"Oh, Father," Jack pleaded as though her life depended on it, "can we discuss this later? Please?"

"Nicholas and I weren't in church this morning because of colds. We feel the need to be updated." Ethan had a playful smirk dancing across his friendly face. "If my wife is still getting grounded by her father at age twenty-eight, something definitely happened that we should know about."

"Nicholas is two," Andy stated in a flat voice. "Two-year-olds do not need to be updated."

"Well, I'm thirty-two," Ethan said, smiling flirtatiously at his wife. "Thirty-two-year-olds definitely need to be updated."

"You're a pest." Andy tossed her linen napkin at him.

"Now, that's nothing new to you, Dear." Ethan took his wife's napkin and spread it out in his lap. "And, by the way, thanks for the napkin. I can always use another one. I tend to run on the messy side."

Andy made a funny face at her husband, and then addressed the steaming question as carefully as she could. "Let's just say that Pastor Bishop wasn't exactly what Jack had in mind for Sugar Creek."

Jack refused to look at anyone. Her face felt so red by now, she was sure it was glowing.

"And just what is that supposed to mean?" Bradley inquired impatiently.

"Nothing. Nothing, really." Sam tried to calm down her future brother-in-law. "We just put a different image in Jack's mind. Well, what I'm trying to say is that it really wasn't her fault."

"What, precisely, wasn't her fault?" Bradley stared at Sam intently. "I want to know what happened."

"Nothing happened," Jack insisted, putting a hand on Bradley's arm. "This whole thing is getting blown out of proportion."

Jack glanced quickly in Matthew's direction, only to find the young pastor sitting back in his chair, looking like he was having the time of his life. He looked at Jack, and then simply smiled more widely. It looked to Jack as though he were trying very hard to suppress his laughter. The fact that he was enjoying himself immensely was far too evident.

"Oh, now calm yourself, Son," Roy Hobson's voice soothingly sounded from the other end of the table. "You know what it's like when all the girls sit together. A few giggles are bound to escape. They can't help it."

"Yeah, you think they'd never seen a handsome feller before," Ray ran a hand through his gray hair in an exaggerated way. "You'd think by now, with Roy and me around, the girls would be plenty used to good-looking fellers." He paused, and then said in a surprised tone, "I guess I was wrong."

The laughter went on, and so did the subject. Shortly after dessert was served, Jack was able to slip out through the kitchen door. She took the narrow servants' stairs up to her bedroom and promptly burst into tears once the door was closed. She felt so humiliated. How on earth had she let this happen? She paused for a moment, as she grabbed her jeans to change into. How had she let what happen? What had happened? As she slipped on her blue canvas sneakers, it suddenly dawned on her that maybe she shouldn't investigate this situation too much. Opening this box could be worse than opening Pandora's box.

"Just leave it alone, Jack," she calmly coaxed herself. "Leave it alone, and maybe it will go away." Yet in her heart, she knew it wouldn't. Issues like this don't die out; they grow with a pace and fury like a hurricane.

After the dinner guests cleared out, she said a quick good-bye to Bradley, and gladly started on the list of chores she had gotten from her father. Blessings do come in strange ways.

As she studied her list, it really wasn't so bad. Her job was to help ready the waterfront for the upcoming tourist season. It was the beginning of April, and all the boats had to be dragged out of the boathouse, cleaned, and then docked. Andy and Jay would be helping as well. Sam had been assigned to garden duty. That was her thing, and Jack was glad to let her have it. Working with the boats was Jack's passion. Out of all the sisters, she was the one who could never get enough of the water or sailing.

As Jack wheeled a catamaran down to the beach, her eight-month-old Mountain Dog, Flyer, tagged after her. Flyer was great company and would often go sailing with Jack. He loved the water as much as she did and never wanted to be left on land.

As Jack was vigorously scrubbing the pontoons of the cat, Flyer began to bark. Flyer was still young, so his bark was high-pitched and very non-threatening. But just the same, the energetic pup did serve as a good doorbell. As Jack popped her head up curiously, she immediately saw Matthew Bishop approaching her. He had changed into an old sweat-shirt and jeans and looked very comfortable.

"I thought I might come by and give you a hand." His voice was kind, but Jack noticed that his eyes were full of laughter.

Jack studied him no longer than a few seconds before she realized his offer was genuine. "You really don't have to. You're not the one being pun-ished here."

Matthew's gentle laughter floated through the air. "Working with boats is no punishment for me. I'm part sea dog."

Jack threw a sponge his way, and he began scrubbing down the opposite pontoon. "Pastor Bishop," Jack began hesitantly, "I'm very sorry about what happened this morning. I hope you realize we weren't laughing at you."

"First of all," Matthew's voice was laid-back, "you should call me Matthew. That's what everyone has always called me. Besides, when you call me Pastor Bishop, I find myself looking around for my Dad."

"Your Dad is a pastor?" Jack asked, instantly intrigued.

"Yup," Matthew smiled and dunked the sponge in some soapy water.

"Where are you from?" Jack asked, popping her head over the top of the cat.

"I guess you weren't there the Sunday the church voted me in," Matthew laughed lightly. "I felt like all of Sugar Creek knew more about me than I knew about myself. It was a strange feeling."

Jack smiled. "It's like that in a small town. Your life is under constant scrutiny. Especially," Jack added thoughtfully, "by the Hobson brothers. They've made an art out of watching people. They are a very observant surveillance team. You'd be wise to watch out for them. They can be simply awful."

Matthew nodded and laughed. "Thanks for the warning." Matthew paused, and patted Flyer for a moment. Jack smiled watching the two together. Now she could see that she and Matthew had at least three things in common. They both loved God. They both loved sailing, and they both loved dogs. She shook her head slowly. Not that she was making a list, the list of things in common was sort of making itself.

Matthew's voice broke through her thoughts. "I'm from Minnesota." He picked up the sponge and began scrubbing the cat again. "My Dad pastors a church in the St. Paul area. I spent most of my life there."

"So why did you come east?" Jack asked in a puzzled voice. "You must miss your family."

"I do miss my family," Matthew said honestly, "but I knew God was calling me to Sugar Creek. It was something I was quite certain of."

"That's good." Jack admired the young pastor's desire to follow God's calling.

"By the way," Matthew brought his head up just enough to look directly into Jack's eyes, "I have a strong feeling that you were set up today. I haven't figured out all the details yet," he added curiously, as his eyes twinkled mischievously, "but I know a set up when I see one."

Before Jack could answer, Andy and Jay pulled a paddleboat out of the boathouse. They dragged it alongside of the catamaran, breathing heavily.

"You're right, Pastor Bishop," Andy laughed. "Jack was set up. I guess you could say this family has a lot of fun. Sometimes," Andy said reflectively, "we get into a lot of trouble for some of our fun." She laughed, and then continued talking easily.

"It's just harmless stuff, really, but there are times that our judgment is not always the best."

"So, what was the set up?" Matthew's smile had grown ear to ear.

"We told Jack that the new pastor was old, bald, and really, really fat," Jay volunteered freely.

As the girls broke up laughing, Matthew had to join them. "Now I understand the look of utter astonishment on your face," Matthew said between fits of laughter. "I'm not that old, and not that fat, and not that bald," he said putting a hand to his hair.

"Oh, you're a total hunk," Jay added quickly. "If you weren't, we never would have teased you." Jay paused, and in a serious tone asked Matthew, "Is it OK that I called you a hunk. I mean, you being a Pastor and all. I didn't mean any disrespect."

Everyone broke up laughing except for Jay. "Hey! I'm serious!"

"No disrespect taken, Jay." Matthew found the sisters very amusing. "I'll take all the good things you said as compliments."

Jack liked Matthew's easygoing personality. The fact that he cared about people was evident. She immediately knew Matthew was going to be a great blessing to Sugar Creek. He was clearly a very special person.

The four of them talked easily the rest of the afternoon as they cleaned and readied the boats. At the end of the day, Andy made them all turkey sandwiches and apple pie.

Late that night, as Jack lay in her bed, her mind recapping the day's events, her thoughts continually turned back to Matthew Bishop. In many ways, he and Bradley were total opposites. Bradley wanted to pastor a large church, while Matthew had purposely chosen a small one. Bradley was confident to the point of being arrogant. Matthew was confident, and comfortable with himself in a very laid-back way. He didn't flaunt himself. He simply was himself and very easy for others to be around. Matthew loved the water and sailing. Bradley disliked both. Jack could never figure out how someone who had grown up on a lake as beautiful as Eagle Lake could dislike the water. Also, Matthew had already formed a friendship with Flyer, while Bradley went out of his way to avoid the dog. He didn't like animals of any kind. She had always thought that was a bit strange.

She did admit to herself that as the wedding date grew closer, she grew more nervous. Even though she had known Bradley most of her life, at times she felt as though she didn't know him at all. He was selective about what he would share with her, and this had always made it difficult to know exactly what he was thinking. They didn't have a lot in common. She secretly acknowledged that.

Yet they did both love the Lord with all their hearts. They wanted to serve Him full-time. Yet one nagging thought persistently bothered her. Was this factor alone enough to make a marriage work?

Jack had to keep reminding herself that she had only known Matthew Bishop for one day. Yet she also knew in her heart, it was a day that would never end for her. It would remain in her heart forever. It was one that her mind would replay again and again. She knew she needed to replay it again. She needed to try to figure out exactly what had happened to her heart.

Four

Two weeks later, on a sunny Monday morning, the Miller girls were busy at the Inn. Monday was always washday, and Sam, Jay, and Jack had been assigned as chambermaids to the upstairs guest rooms. The Victorian inn was a large, white, sprawling structure, with green shutters and plenty of nooks and crannies decorating it. On the outside, there were long, wide, white porches, with spindle railings gracing the front and back of the Inn. The porches were lined with white, wooden rocking chairs and always looked very inviting, regardless of the weather or temperature.

On the inside, the Inn was decorated in appropriate Victorian style. Highly polished wooden floors, grandfather clocks, stained-glass lamps, bubble lamps, Tiffany lamps, Oriental rugs, and antiques of every kind, some genuine, and some not so genuine, decorated the Inn.

The Miller family had managed to keep a delicate balance between the Victorian ambiance and down-to-earth, everyday comfort. The chairs were meant to be sat in, the couches were meant to be crowded with people holding food and drinks, and the antique coffee tables were meant to have legs draping across them. The Inn was stylish, but designed to be lived in. Max Miller often told his guests the Inn was not a museum. He would tell folks it was not only his home, but also their home for the stay.

The Inn consisted of ten guest bedrooms, a large, airy country kitchen, a formal dining room, a game room, a spacious den, a library full of the classics, and the family's living quarters. The family's favorite room, by far, was Clancy's. Clancy's was a small eatery decorated like an English tavern. It had a long counter at one end of the room with black metal stools in front of it and several booths and wooden tables scattered throughout the rest of it. The Inn would serve its guests a hearty breakfast, and Clancy's was designed to provide light dinners of soup, salad, and sandwiches. At capacity, Clancy's could hold sixty-five people, and it was usually filled to overflowing. With Mother and Andy cooking, both of whom had graduated from culinary school, Clancy's had a well-earned reputation for delicious food. People came from miles around just to eat there.

As Jack, Jay, and Sam worked as chambermaids in the ten guest bedrooms, they talked and teased each other freely. "That sure was nice of

Matthew to come and help us ready the waterfront. It's such a huge job. I know Father has really appreciated his help." Sam spoke sincerely as she began stripping the sheets off the canopy bed she was assigned to.

"So did Jack," Jay added in a frisky tone, as she tugged the sheets from a double bed across the hall. "I think she appreciated it more than anyone!"

"And just what is that supposed to mean?" Jack demanded, as she scooped up a load of dirty towels in her arms.

"Whatever you want it to mean." Jay was annoyingly evasive.

"What are you talking about?" Jack demanded, dropping her towels and entering the room that Jay was working in.

Jay tossed the dirty sheets into the corner of the room, and then turned to face her younger sister directly. "I don't think you want to know what I mean," she stated in an even tone.

"Yes, I do." The anger was mounting in Jack's voice.

"I think you and Matthew make a cute couple," Jay burst out laughing, "but you'd better make sure you have fire insurance, Girl, because you're going to get burned big time. You can't date two guys at the same time. Everyone knows that!"

"What are you talking about?" Jack threw her hands on her hips defensively. "I have no idea what planet you come from."

"It's not hard to get ideas watching you and Matthew," Jay's tone was matter-of-fact. "You two complement each other nicely. You're good together."

"We are not together!" Jack spat out angrily. "I've only known the man for a few weeks. There is no way we could be together!" Jack sighed in frustration. "Besides, I'm already in a relationship with Bradley. Remember him?"

"I wish I couldn't!" Jay moaned regretfully, rolling her eyes at her sister for added effect. "I wish you'd forget about him. He's a first-class loser. You deserve better, Jack."

Sam threw a hand over Jack's mouth quickly. "Listen, knock it off, you two. We're never going to finish cleaning these rooms if you two don't stop fighting."

"We're not fighting," Jay pointed out quickly. "We're discussing. I'm simply making a few candid observations about Jack's life." Jay turned and looked at Jack, and said in a shocked tone, "I honestly thought she'd appreciate it."

Jack's mouth dropped open, yet no words came out. Jay certainly knew how to get under her skin and push all the right buttons to make her blow. She cleared her throat slowly, and then said as calmly as she could, "Why don't you stick to observing your own life."

"It's not nearly as interesting as yours!" Jay looked at Jack smugly. "Two men and one lost, confused chick...now that's interesting. A real-life drama unfolding before my very eyes! This is great!"

"I'm taking the dirty towels downstairs to the laundry," Jack stated in a voice that she was trying hard to keep under control. "I'll pick up the clean towels, and then come back up." Turning to look at Jay, she said in a warning tone, "The subject had better be changed before I get back up here."

Jack bent down, and picked up an enormous pile of dirty towels. "You're not taking all those in one trip, are you?" Sam asked in a concerned voice. "You're going to end up dumping them all over the stairs."

"I'm fine," Jack mumbled as she turned to go.

As Jack waddled down the long, narrow hallway, Roy Hobson came out of his room. "Are you looking for a challenge there, Jack?" He laughed at the load she was carrying. She was barely managing to hold all the towels together. "Or maybe you're simply trying to set a new world's record."

"I'm fine." Jack was already struggling from the strain of the load. She was too proud to admit defeat.

"Of course you're fine," Roy agreed in his usual laid-back voice. "You're always fine."

Jack was especially close to Roy. They had a special friendship and enjoyed each other's company immensely. Roy was someone that Jack could talk to, and he was someone that she could trust with her secrets. She often confided in the older man and sought out his advice in many areas.

"What's eating you, Jack? It looks to me like you've got yourself a bee in your bonnet. Is that Jay teasing you again?"

"I'm fine," Jack answered again quickly, as she stumbled into the narrow servants' staircase. The stairs were old and shorter than standard steps. The staircase was difficult to maneuver at best. Jack realized too late that it was going to be impossible with such a huge load of towels. Whether she would verbally admit defeat or not seemed entirely unimportant at this moment. She knew that she was going down and defeat was about to claim her, regardless of what she was willing to admit.

As her footing slipped on the slim, board steps, the towels, as well as Jack, went flying down the stairs to the kitchen below, with all the grace of an avalanche. As she landed with a thud on the hard kitchen floor, she immediately took inventory of the situation. She was truly surprised she wasn't dead, or at the very least, severely injured.

Just as her survey was complete, she heard a strained, muffled voice from below her. "Could you please get off me?"

As she rolled off the pile of towels she had landed on, a very rumpled-looking Matthew Bishop dug himself out from underneath the load. The expression on his face was one of mixed bewilderment, shock, and unbridled pain.

It was at that moment that Max Miller and his wife Melina came running into the kitchen. "What happened in here?" they shouted in unison, as they surveyed the scattered towels, as well as the people lying on the floor.

"Looks like she totally flattened the new pastor," Ray Hobson said in an amused tone, as he observed the scene from the breakfast nook. With coffee and muffin in hand, he eyeballed the whole sight again and again. "I've heard of dinner theater," he chuckled, "but never breakfast theater. Good show, Jack."

Roy, who had followed the avalanche down the stairs, shook his head in bewilderment. "She very nearly annihilated Pastor Bishop. Are you OK there, Son?" Roy asked the pastor sympathetically.

"I'm fine," Matthew answered slowly. "I'm fine."

"Another one that's fine," Roy mumbled, shaking his bald head.

"Pastor, I'm so sorry," Max apologized as he helped the disheveled man to his feet. "Are you hurt at all?"

"No, Max," Matthew replied firmly. "I'm fine."

"Fine again," Roy shook his head and laughed. "Everybody's fine. Isn't that nice?" He paused thoughtfully. "What is it with young people and that word today?"

For the first time since his near-death experience, Matthew gazed around the room. Towels had landed not only on the floor, but in the sink, on the counters, on the two dogs, and even on Ray Hobson's lap. Matthew smiled and then let loose a low, rumbling laugh. Soon everyone was laughing. Everyone, that is, except for Jack. She was biting her bottom lip and looking as though she were trying hard not to cry.

"Jack," Matthew said gently, "it's OK. I'm all right." Then he extended his hand, and helped her up.

At his very touch, Jack felt a feeling that she had never experienced before. A warmth surged from his hand to hers and then throughout her entire body. It was electrifying and numbing at the same time and left Jack feeling at a complete loss. She quickly searched Matthew's face and could tell by the puzzled expression there that he had felt the same feeling, too. He awkwardly dropped her hand and took a step back.

As the silence in the room thickened, Roy cleared his throat loudly. "I'll tell you, as sure as the sun shines, there is never a dull moment here at the Sugar Creek Inn. Absolutely never."

That snapped Jack out of her trance, and she immediately sprang into action. She began gathering up the scattered towels at a furious pace. She didn't dare look anyone in the eye; her emotions were too out-of-control for that. She tried to rein them back in and leave the kitchen as quickly as possible, yet she felt it was a mission impossible. She knew she wouldn't break free that easily.

Max offered Matthew a steaming cup of coffee, which the young pastor gladly accepted. "Tell me, Matthew, what brings you to the Inn this fine Monday morning?"

"I had told Ray that I would bring a book by for him," Matthew raked a hand through his disarrayed hair.

"Bet you never thought you should take out life insurance before you came!" Ray mumbled quietly, with a distinct twinkle in his eye.

"Have you seen much of the lake yet? Eagle Lake is sure one of God's special creations," Max said fondly, as he offered Matthew a blueberry muffin.

Matthew waved the muffin off politely before answering. "I've been so busy that I've only seen a tiny part of the lake — between my house and yours."

"Well, that settles it now, doesn't it?" Max patted the young man on the back. "I'm going to supply you with the best sailor and tour guide on the lake. She knows about the history of the lake, as well as all the people and the islands. It will be perfect."

"That sounds great!" Matthew agreed enthusiastically.

"Jack should be finished by one," Max said, focusing in on the pile of towels she had collected. "Why don't you stop by then?"

Matthew looked uncertainly at the young woman with the long brown ponytail swinging, as she was bending to pick up towels. She froze at the sound of her name, but quickly composed herself. When she spoke, Matthew couldn't help but notice that she had a definite alternative plan in mind.

"Wouldn't Eddie be better for this, Father? Matthew could ride the mail boat route and meet most of the people on the lake." Jack had tried to sound carefree, but she knew her voice had revealed the strain she felt inside.

"No, Jack." Max spoke firmly to his daughter. "You nearly killed the man. You more than owe him."

"One o'clock is good for me." Jack glanced at Matthew and then quickly returned to her pile of towels.

"Uh, Jack..." Matthew's voice filled with hesitation, "it's really not necessary. I can see you're busy. Maybe some other time."

"Oh, yes, it is necessary," Max stated in an unyielding tone.

Jack put down her towels for a minute and looked up at Matthew. "I really don't mind, if you don't. I love this lake and I love to sail. I'll bring along Sam and Flyer. We'll have fun."

"If you're sure you don't mind," Matthew asked, with excitement mounting in his voice.

"I'd love to. See you at one." Jack forced a smile at the young pastor just before she turned and left the room.

Matthew turned to Roy excitedly. "I haven't been sailing since last summer. I can't wait."

"Do you know how to swim, Son?" Roy asked in a serious tone.

"I learned to swim as a boy," Matthew answered curiously, scrunching up his face. "Why do you ask?"

"When Jack's the captain of the vessel, I find it a skill that comes in handy." Roy couldn't hold back his laughter any longer. "What she calls sailing, I basically think of as swimming. It's kind of the same thing with Jack."

"You'd better pick yourself up a roll or two of duct tape, Matthew," Ray added in a matter-of-fact tone. "That's as important as knowing how to swim when you're sailing with Jack."

Five

$\mathcal{A}$s Matthew stood on the wooden dock patting Flyer and watching Jack prepare her catamaran for sailing, he instantly understood why Roy and Ray had asked him if he knew how to swim. He also understood the reference to the duct tape. It appeared, at a quick glance, that at least a quarter of the boat was being held together by the shiny, silver tape. The sight was neither comforting nor inviting. To say that the old cat was unseaworthy seemed like a vast understatement. It was probably some sort of miracle that the boat hadn't sunk by now. The fact that it was actually floating amazed him.

After a more careful inspection, Matthew noticed several good-sized holes in the cat's pontoons. He glanced at the duct tape in his hands and doubted seriously if the tape would help those holes. They looked beyond repair.

He closed his eyes for a minute, trying quickly to formulate a logical-sounding excuse. The first thing that came to his mind was that he was too young to die. This reason was true, yet he knew it would anger Jack, so he searched his mind for something more acceptable.

When he opened his eyes again, Jack was staring at him with a comical expression on her face. "It really does sail well. She's the fastest cat on the lake."

"I guess I wasn't exactly concerned about the speed." Matthew spoke hesitantly. How could he put this kindly? "It's just that your boat…"

"Looks worn a bit," Jack finished his trailing sentence as she readied her sails. "Pastor Bishop," Jack challenged, "you, of all people, should know that you shouldn't judge a book by its cover."

"Uh…we're not talking about a book here, Jack," Matthew replied slowly. "And from here, it does look like your boat is basically being held together by duct tape." He paused momentarily, and ran an agitated hand through his hair. "It's disturbing, to put it mildly."

Just then, Sam passed him on the dock and jumped onto the boat. "It looks like it's being held together with duct tape because it is!" Sam laughed hard.

Jack just scowled at her. She was very protective of her boat. She understood why people made fun of it, yet she simply didn't like it.

"Oh," Sam tried to quickly cover her remarks, "it is a really good boat. It's fast, and, uh, and a really good boat."

Jack glared at her sister, and then turned her attention toward Matthew. "If you'd rather not go, I understand," her voice was tight. "And," she said matter-of-factly, as she started rigging the sail, "I know my cat is not the best-looking boat. She has seen a lot of years. She was handed down to me by my grandfather. He taught me how to sail and swim. This boat holds a lot of wonderful memories for me. I intend to keep sailing her until she sinks."

Matthew fought to contain his laughter, but lost. "That may happen very soon," he said laughing loudly. Sam joined him in laughter, but Jack threw her hands on her hips angrily and stared him down.

"I'm sorry, Jack," Matthew tried to sound sincere, yet the laughter that kept escaping from his lips didn't help his cause. "She's just not what I expected."

"Do you do only things that you expect to?"

"No. Of course not."

"Then live dangerously for once." Jack grabbed the rudder in one hand, and the rope in the other. "Come aboard."

"Well," he hopped aboard the floating disaster, "I do know how to swim, and I do know that I'm going to heaven when I die."

"You're a wise guy, Pastor," Jack smirked at him, as she tightened the sail. Instantly, as though she had jammed the accelerator, the wind filled the sail, and the old cat took off. Matthew had to admit the pick-up on the boat was impressive.

As they soared across Eagle Lake, Matthew's face took on the excitement of a child's at Christmas. "I love this," he smiled broadly in Jack's direction. "This," he waved a hand across the lake, "is worth staring death in the face."

"I'll take that as a compliment," Jack smiled back at him. "Sailing always makes me feel so free. I can always lose my troubles out here. This old cat makes me feel like I'm flying."

"Is that why you named your pup Flyer?" Matthew asked, stroking the Mountain Dog's head.

"Yes," Jack glanced lovingly at her dog. "His name reminds me of where I like to be the most — flying across Eagle Lake."

"Has Flyer been sailing with you long?" Matthew watched the pup relax and curl up on the trampoline as though he intended to go to sleep. "He couldn't look more comfortable even if he were lying before a warm fireplace."

Jack laughed warmly at his comment. "Flyer has been sailing with me since he was eight weeks old." Jack paused for a moment, smiling thoughtfully at the memory. "I only had two problems teaching Flyer how to be a good mate. First, I had to teach him not to jump off the boat to chase the fish. And second, I had to teach him not to bark at other boats as we passed them on the lake."

Matthew laughed. "So, I guess he's a little protective of his lake."

Jack and Sam both laughed this time. "Flyer is very protective of Eagle Lake. He thinks the lake is an extension of his own back yard. In his doggy mind, he thinks he owns the lake," Jack said with a wide grin on her face. "But now he's coming to realize that he has to share it."

"Does Docker like to sail?" Matthew asked, referring to the Inn's other Mountain Dog.

"No," Jack answered quickly.

Sam laughed, and Matthew eyed her expectantly, waiting for the story. "That's because Jack has dumped that poor old dog in the lake one too many times."

"You're kidding?" The level of concern in Matthew's voice skyrocketed.

"That is one of the risks of sailing," Jack stated defensively. "Sometimes you misjudge the wind, and she flips over your boat. It happens to the best of us." She stared at Matthew defiantly, and then said in a bold voice, "If you don't want to get wet, you shouldn't play with water."

Matthew's eyes bugged out, and he wasn't sure how to reply to his feisty captain. "OK…"

Sam laughed. "Yeah, but Jack has a reputation for dumping her passengers in the lake quite often. A lot of people won't sail with her anymore."

Matthew raised his eyebrows at Sam. "It's probably late to be asking...but is there something I should know here?"

Sam laughed again. "I guess it's a bit late to warn you about our captain, but I'll tell you it's very unwise to upset her when she's at the helm. If I were you, I wouldn't get into any heated discussions with her out here on the lake."

"And why is that?" Matthew asked, clearly intrigued.

"She'll tip the boat just enough so you get dumped into the lake. She's a pro at lifting the pontoon out of the water just enough to slide her rival off the trampoline. Jack's very good at it."

"And don't you just think that was something you should have told me before I boarded her boat?" Matthew shook his head comically. "I can assure you that I would have been extremely interested in that little tidbit of news."

Amazingly, Jack hadn't said a word either way. She seemed to be ignoring the entire conversation. Her eyes were focused far out on the water, yet somehow Matthew knew her ears were tuned in to the current conversation.

"Is this all true?" he asked her frankly.

Jack turned, and then stared at Matthew directly. With her long ponytail blowing in the breeze, she appeared innocent enough. Yet, at the same time, her wide, audacious smile told a completely different story. It was all the confirmation he needed.

"It is true, isn't it?"

"Relax, Matthew," Jack laughed quietly. "Sam's just having fun with you."

"You mean to tell me that you've never dumped anyone off your boat?" he demanded.

Jack's smile faded, and her eyes narrowed slightly. "Accidents do happen."

With that said, Jack turned her full attention back to the lake. Matthew had his answer. Tread carefully when you're on Jack's boat. The thought troubled him because he knew he tended to be confrontational at times. He often spoke the truth, whether it was in his best interest or not. A smile spread across his face as he realized how glad he was that he knew how to swim well.

"We're approaching Blueberry Island." Jack grew excited. "It's my favorite island on the lake."

"How many islands are on Eagle Lake?" Matthew asked interestedly.

"Four," Jack answered quickly. "There's Big Bear, Moose Head, Pine Tree, and then Blueberry."

"Why do you like Blueberry the best?"

Jack smiled at the question. "Blueberry is the biggest of the four islands. She has a lot of variety—gently rolling hills, trees, ponds, streams, and a meadow loaded with blueberry bushes."

"Sounds great!" Matthew's enthusiasm was growing by the minute. "Can we go exploring?"

"I'd love to!" Jack answered eagerly, as she steered her cat into a sandy beach cove.

As the three of them struggled to pull the cat up on the beach, Flyer playfully chased the fish. Everyone laughed at the sight. "I don't think he'd know what to do with a fish if he actually caught one. It would probably be the shock of his life," Jack said, calling Flyer to her.

As the three of them started down the path that would lead them into the center of the island, the rumbling sound of a motorboat could be heard off in the distance. Sam turned, and her face immediately lit up as she recognized the boat.

"It's Eddie!" Sam immediately turned and walked toward the beach to meet him. Flyer, who was still in the water looking for fish, started wagging his tail, sending water spraying everywhere.

Jack turned to Matthew. "Eddie Peck and Sam have been good friends for a long time. He's the mailman on the lake. When the weather permits, he often delivers his route by motorboat.

"Are Sam and Eddie dating?" Matthew asked as he studied the approaching boat.

Jack smiled. "Eddie's too shy to ask Sam out. They do a lot of stuff together as friends. They really enjoy each other's company."

"That's good," Matthew nodded.

"I think so." Jack glanced lovingly at her sister.

"I thought I recognized your boat," Eddie shouted over to Jack. "There's not many boats on the lake like Jack's," Eddie stated, as he slipped on his hip-high fisherman boots and waded through the knee-deep water to the beach. Flyer gave him a presidential greeting, and Eddie spent a few moments playing with the pup.

After the girls introduced Eddie to Matthew, Eddie turned to Sam shyly. "I was sort of hoping you might want to help me deliver my route today. The load seems heavier than normal."

Sam smiled shyly back at him. "I'd like that."

"I'll drop her back at the Inn later."

Jack nodded. " I'll let my Dad know. Have fun."

As Eddie turned to go, he suddenly stopped and faced Matthew. "I think I should warn you," he said to the young pastor nervously, "Jack has hit some rocks with her boat."

"I noticed the holes," Matthew replied seriously.

"It really wasn't her fault," Eddie rattled on. "Just to let you know," he continued on in an anxious tone, "she doesn't like to be made fun of. Don't call her names like Captain Crunch." Eddie glanced quickly in Jack's direction. "She doesn't see the humor in it, and she may toss you in the lake."

Matthew nodded and then smiled. Jack did have quite a reputation. He instantly wondered if Eddie had been one of her victims. "Thanks for the warning, Eddie. It was nice to meet you."

Jack and Matthew watched Sam and Eddie take off. Then Jack turned to her new friend and said excitedly, "Are you ready to see the island?"

"I love to explore!" Matthew sounded like a kid again.

As Jack and Flyer led Matthew down a pine-covered path into the forest, Jack couldn't help but think of how different Matthew and Bradley were. About the only thing they did have in common, besides being men, was their call to the pulpit.

"You're awfully quiet," Matthew's tone was sensitive.

"Oh, I was just thinking."

"You see," Matthew continued on easily, "being shorter than you does have its advantages."

"Oh?" Jack turned sideways to look at him.

"Yes," Matthew said smiling up at her, "I have a clear view of your face."

"Ah…" Jack said, wondering where this conversation was leading.

"And from here," Matthew smiled up at her, "it looks like your mind is going a mile a minute."

Jack laughed softly. "I guess it is."

"If you want to share, I'm a great listener," Matthew said in a heartfelt way.

"I can see that about you," Jack admitted as she sat down on a fallen tree. Matthew sat down next to her, grabbed a stick, and began drawing in the dirt with it. He was amusing to watch. His excitement about being on the island was so pure and child-like.

"I was just thinking about Bradley." Jack grew even more quiet.

At that moment, Flyer noticed that they weren't following him anymore. He turned and looked back at them with confusion clearly written across his fuzzy face. It was obvious that he wanted to explore, not hang around.

"What's Bradley like?" Matthew asked, still fiddling with his stick.

"Well, you met him at lunch the first Sunday you were here," Jack tried to sound nonchalant.

"Yeah, but it wasn't for very long," Matthew said smiling up at her. "And, since I am supposed to marry the two of you, I think a little background info is in order here."

Jack turned abruptly and stared at the young pastor with a wrinkled-up face. "What do you mean by 'supposed to'?"

"You know, I'm the new pastor at Eagle Lake Bible Chapel. I'm supposed to marry you and Bradley."

Jack stared at him again for a second and then turned and absent-mindedly watched Flyer take off after a squirrel. "I know who you are, Pastor," Jack narrowed her eyes at him, "but what I don't know is why you used the word 'supposed.'"

"What's wrong with it?" Matthew asked in a laid-back tone.

"It implies doubt. It suggests that you might not marry us," Jack's voice had inadvertently taken on a worried tone.

"Are you having doubts?" Matthew quickly searched Jack's stormy face.

As he targeted her with his intriguing brown eyes, Jack panicked. She felt like she couldn't hide anything from those inquisitive eyes. "No," she tried to sound as confident as she could. She jumped off the log and swiftly started moving down the pine path. "It's time for you to see the rest of the island."

"I didn't mean to get you mad, Jack." Matthew's voice held confusion.

"I know," Jack answered quietly. "It's not your fault." Then, under her breath, she mumbled, "but, in a way, it is your fault."

Matthew grabbed her arm, forcing her to stop walking away from him. "What do you mean by that?" His tone had taken on urgency. "What's going on here, Jack? Please talk to me."

Flyer returned, looking for something to chase. Jack picked up a large stick, and tossed it as far as she could into the forest. Flyer anxiously took off after it.

Jack looked at Matthew for a moment and then nodded. As she sat down on a large gray rock, she spoke in a voice that was filled with anguish. "Matthew," she sighed deeply, as she twisted her fingers restlessly, "I don't believe I've ever met anyone like you before."

"And," Matthew's voice held uncertainty, "that's a good thing?"

Jack laughed and then began to relax a little. "Yes, Matthew. That's a very good thing. You are a very special person. You have a depth of compassion and care for others that I've never witnessed before. I…" Jack choked up and couldn't go on.

Matthew knelt down in front of her, and put a loving hand on her shoulder. "Jack, what's this really all about? I mean," his voice was tentative, "I appreciate the compliment. Don't get me wrong, but I have a feeling that there's a lot more behind what you're saying."

"Matthew, I'm going to be honest with you." Jack fiddled nervously with the end of her coat.

"Honesty is good."

"Have you ever met someone and known them for a short time, yet felt in your heart that you've known them all your life? You just seem to connect with them on a deep level and feel more comfortable with them than anyone else you've ever met. It's almost like," Jack paused searching for the right words, "like, your heart has come home."

Matthew waited for her to look directly into his eyes, and when she did, he held them with his own a second before answering. "Yes, Jack, I have. I know exactly what you mean," his voice had grown husky with emotion.

"Well…" Jack fought for control over her emotions. "I don't think I can go on."

"Please do," Matthew urged.

"I can't." Jack wiped away the tears running down her cheeks. "It's getting late, and you should see some of the island before we have to go."

"I'd rather listen to what you have on your heart."

He was so easy-going and non-threatening that Jack knew that if she stayed with him much longer, she would end up revealing the unedited miniseries of her life story to him. "You're too easy to talk to, Matthew," Jack whispered, fighting the whirling emotions within her. "And to be honest with you, I feel too confused by my own emotions to talk."

As they started walking, Matthew spoke in a caring tone, "You know what I do, when I'm feeling like you?"

Jack stopped, and turned to look at him. " No. What?"

"I pray," Matthew's voice had become earnest. "God knows my thoughts anyway…so I might as well come clean before Him. I put the confusion into His hands and ask Him to help me straighten it out."

Jack began to walk again, and Matthew silently came beside her. "That's good advice, Pastor. I think I'll take you up on that."

"Good," Matthew nodded thoughtfully.

They walked on for several minutes in silence before Matthew noticed a log cabin in the clearing ahead. "Someone lives on Blueberry Island?" Surprise was written all over his face.

Jack laughed softly. "I wish I did. That's the Eagle Lake Rangers' emergency shelter. If you're out on the lake and you get caught in a storm, you can stay there."

"That's nice." Matthew walked toward the small log cabin.

"It really is," Jack agreed following after him. "They keep it stocked with wood for the fireplace and basic food for the kitchen."

"It sounds like a free vacation."

"You can get arrested if you use the cabin for anything other than emergencies. The Rangers love this place and monitor it pretty closely."

Jack was relieved for the change of subject. She felt her heart do odd things around Matthew. She was not only alarmed by her feelings, but confused by them as well. Never in her life had she experienced such sensations of the heart. She wanted to kick herself. She belonged to Bradley, yet recently she needed to continually remind herself of that. A thought persisted in the back of her mind. It was a nagging thought, and she particularly hated nagging thoughts. They forced her out of her comfort zone. They made her confront areas in her life that she had neatly buried and didn't want to deal with. Yet the thought endured. It refused to leave. The thought that plagued her mind again and again was, if her heart really belonged to Bradley, why did she have to work so hard at remembering that?

"You're off on me again," Matthew laughed. "Taking another sixty second vacation, Jack?"

"I'm sorry, Matthew," Jack said sincerely.

"You don't have to be sorry," Matthew said gen-uinely. "But you should remember that I'm always here for you. Remember…" Matthew spread his hands wide, "the good listener thing and all."

Jack laughed. "Thanks again."

As they continued on, they came to a huge meadow. Half was filled with rather shabby-look-ing bushes. "Too bad those old, tattered, weather-beaten bushes are taking over the meadow." Matthew eyed them with disdain.

"Matthew," Jack placed a friendly hand on his arm, "those are blueberry bushes! They produce some of the best blueberries in all of Maine—and they're free!"

"The bushes don't look appealing at all." Matthew stared at the rows and rows of blueberry bushes.

"That's OK," Jack laughed. "We're not eating the bushes! We're eating the berries, and the berries are very appealing. Hey," Jack put her hand on Matthew's arm again, "I bet there's a ser-mon illustration in there somewhere."

Matthew laughed at her. "So, are you starting to help me write my sermons, Miss Miller?"

"No, not at all. But," Jack wiggled her eye-brows at him, "I'll give you plenty of advice—for free, of course."

Once again Matthew laughed. "You know, when they say the best things in life are for free, somehow I can almost guarantee they weren't talking about advice. Advice is heaped out on people like it's some kind of grand blessing. Something we should be eternally grateful for. And," Matthew added, shaking his head slightly, "I am very grateful for the good advice I've gotten over the years. Yet I've gotten enough bad advice in my time to drown me. And," he laughed loudly, "then the people who gave me the bad advice would say, 'Hey, what are you drowning for? We gave you all that wonderful, free advice!'"

Jack laughed. "Been there. Experienced that. Don't want a return ticket!"

"Hey," Matthew's tone was sharp as he looked toward the blueberry bushes again, "someone has beaten us to Maine's free blueberries." Grabbing Jack's hand, he said in a concerned tone, "Let's get out of here."

Jack laughed softly and sank to the ground behind a large bush. "The bears won't hurt you. They are actually very friendly. Oh, but I do have to admit," Jack went on, with excitement growing in her voice, "this time of year, in the early spring, they do tend to be a little grouchy. They're just waking up from their long winter's nap, and they're skinny and hungry."

"Now the skinny/hungry thing is what concerns me the most. I don't want them staring at me, trying to decide if I would best be suited as an appetizer, entrée, or dessert."

Jack covered her mouth with her hand to muffle her laughter. "You are too funny!"

He smiled back at her, and their eyes locked. For a moment, time stood still. Neither one was aware of the surroundings. They were totally lost in each other's gaze. Jack was vaguely aware of the fact that she wasn't breathing. She felt as though she were under some sort of powerful spell with Matthew, being pulled in further and further by the love she saw in his eyes. The gaze turned into a stare and deepened in intensity. Suddenly the moment was broken by a bear rustling through the bushes near them. It was at that moment that Jack unexpectedly realized she was still tenderly holding Matthew's hand. She looked down at their hands entwined and for a second couldn't tell whose fingers were whose. She shook her head slightly, trying to free her mind of the thick fog that had encompassed her brain. When the inappropriateness of the situation finally dawned on her, it hit her like a ton of bricks. Her face turned a deep shade of red.

"I'm sorry, Matthew." Jack's voice was distant. She dropped his hand as though it had burned her and jumped to her feet.

"It's OK," Matthew replied in a tone filled with bewilderment.

"We should head back," Jack said, speaking too quickly. Nervousness flooded over her as she stumbled quickly down the pine path. This time Matthew didn't walk beside her but walked slowly behind her, with Flyer tagging playfully along.

Jack prayed for a strong wind to take them home quickly. A long ride home with Matthew Bishop would be nothing short of torture. There was something between them that she could no longer deny. It wasn't in her imagination as she had hoped. It was real. It was suddenly all too real.

The only immediate plan Jack could come up with was the "Jack Miller Flight Plan." She would stay away from Matthew as much as she could. The man simply baffled her. He only messed her up when he was around. It made great sense to her to avoid him, and not be around him any more then she had to. She knew it was a full-fledged chicken plan, but as a matter of survival, she would stoop to play the role of a chicken. She wasn't proud when it concerned survival matters. "You do what you have to do, Girl," Jack coached herself. And, what she had to do right now was to stay as far away from Pastor Bishop as she could.

Six

Jack managed to successfully avoid Matthew Bishop for the next several weeks. She slipped out of church using the side entrances, and whenever Matthew stopped by the Inn, she disappeared to an area where she could hide. She knew she was acting like a coward, and she hated herself for it. Yet the array of feelings that the young pastor sent slamming through her was both confusing and alarming. Avoidance seemed like the best plan, yet Jack knew that to pull this off much longer would take nothing short of a miracle.

As Jack leaned against the Inn's old pine registration counter, Sam, Jay, and Andy came bustling into the room. "Hey, I've got a message for you from Pastor Bishop," Andy handed her a white folded note. "He wants to meet you and Bradley for your first marriage counseling session this Saturday at 11:00."

"You read my message!" Jack's tone was clearly accusing.

"Relax, Sweetie, I took the message. I not only read it, but I wrote it, too." Andy came up and dropped an arm around Jack lovingly. "Hey, Little Sister, what's eating you? You haven't been acting like yourself for weeks."

Jack exhaled loudly and shook her head slowly. "Have you ever noticed that life doesn't always work out as planned?"

"It seldom does, Honey." Andy's voice was loving and gentle. "It's good to know that God is in control. His plans for us are often better than anything we could imagine."

"That's true," Jack nodded thoughtfully. Sometimes, lately especially, she felt as though the world were closing in on her. She felt suffocated and trapped. She had purposely been avoiding Matthew and spending more time with Bradley. She talked on the phone with him almost every night. Yet, instead of being a treat, it was becoming more like a dreaded chore. She felt as if she was seeing Bradley in a new light, and she didn't like what she saw. He was driven to the point of walking over anyone around him who got in his way. His attitude could be extremely stubborn and loudly obnoxious. Why she hadn't seen this before, she didn't know. One thing she did know for sure was, this wasn't the type of person that she wanted to spend the rest of her life with. Having Bradley away had not made the heart grow fonder. It had made her heart feel relieved. Having a long-distance relationship with Bradley had been great. She felt sick when she thought about having to be around him all the time after they were married.

"Jack," Sam asked softly, "are you OK?"

How could she explain her feelings to her sisters when she didn't understand them herself?

"Jack?" Jay asked in an alarmed tone, "What's going on? You're walking around as though you're carrying all of life's burdens on your shoulders."

"And you're losing weight," Andy added in a concerned voice. "What's wrong? Aren't my wonderful desserts tempting you any more?"

Jack laughed. "Your desserts are great. And," she added taking the note from Andy's hand, "I'm not losing weight."

"I bet this is about Bradley," Jay mumbled angrily. "He makes me lose my appetite, too." Jay glared hard in Jack's direction. "What's he done now?"

Jack laughed nervously, and shook her head. "Nothing. He's done absolutely nothing."

"And that's the problem," Jay pointed out quickly. "He's always done nothing."

"Father likes him." Jack became defensive.

"Father also thinks there is nothing wrong with wearing two different kinds of plaids together." Andy studied her younger sister closely.

"He also thinks that there is nothing wrong with putting ketchup on ice cream," Sam added quietly.

"I think it's safe to say that, at times, his judgment is not the best."

The girls laughed. "He does have some odd habits," Jack said smiling at her sisters. "Someday we will be able to write an interesting book about old Maxwell Miller."

The sisters talked a few more minutes before they realized they had better get moving on their chores for the day. The beginning of May brought out the pre-tourist crowd. The Inn's ten guest rooms were filled to capacity, which meant a lot of work for the Miller family.

Jack was wishing she could go out for a sail. It always helped her clear her mind. Instead, she had a list of chores a mile long to do and a note in her pocket that weighed more than a cannon ball.

Today, her job was to give Clancy's, the Inn's little restaurant, a thorough cleaning. She was glad Father had assigned her sisters to other areas. She valued the privacy, and it would give her the time she needed to sort through her mixed-up thoughts.

Just as she started dusting the antique oak eating-counter that ran along the front of Clancy's, Roy Hobson came in with his cup of coffee and his morning paper.

"Jack," he said purposefully, "I've got some business to discuss with you. You can keep working, but I want you to hear me out before you start to argue with me."

Jack was a little puzzled by Roy's forceful tone. Ray was usually the pushy one, and Roy was the laid-back brother. This new attitude intrigued Jack, and she popped her head up from behind the counter to look at him.

"Am I going to argue with you, Roy?" Jack asked her elderly friend, in an amused tone.

"Aw...probably, Jack. You're the youngest sister and you tend to get a bit sassy." Roy winked at her over his newspaper.

"What's on your mind?"

"You know I'm not getting any younger..." his voice trailed on quietly.

Jack had to laugh. "None of us are, Roy. Life is kind of irreversible and non-negotiable that way."

"A good point, My Girl," he answered in an amused voice, looking at her with just the trace of a smile hanging on his lips. "But right now we're talking about me. Try to stay focused here, Jack. Will you?"

Jack smiled and nodded at her long-time friend. "OK, Roy. I'll try."

"Good," he said in a satisfied tone and then took a loud gulp of his coffee. Roy and Ray were famous for doing all kinds of strange things to their coffee. Sometimes they'd drop candies into them, such as caramel, chocolate, and butterscotch. Other times they'd add syrups, such as maple, blueberry, or strawberry. Jack stared at Roy's cup wondering which way he had doctored it up this time.

"What I was trying to say before is that I don't know how much longer I'll be driving. I am getting up there, you know."

Jack stopped dusting a booth she had moved into and looked at Roy intently. She couldn't help but wonder where this old coot was going. "Roy," Jack's voice was direct, "I hate to tell you this, but you've been up there for years. What's this really all about?"

Roy gazed at Jack through narrowed eyes for a moment and then directed his attention to his coffee cup. In a quiet but firm voice, he stated, "You need to get back to driving again, Jack."

Jack stood frozen for a minute, staring at Roy in disbelief. As she regained her composure, she looked him directly in the eye, and said calmly, but firmly, "No." The small word carried enough power and conviction so no doubt was left as to her feelings on this matter in the least.

"Well, I believe you do," Roy stated emphatically. "And," he went on determinedly, "I plan to give you driving lessons before all the summer tourists clog up the roadways."

Jack had to laugh at his last comment. "You're used to driving with no cars in front of you or behind you. When you get three cars in front of you, you complain about being in the worst traffic jam in the country." She looked at Roy and simply shook her head. "You are too funny for words."

"Don't try to change the subject, Young Lady," Roy stared at her unwaveringly.

Jack smiled at Roy, and then laughed. "I think I forgot what the subject was."

"Driving lessons," he stated evenly.

"I don't need them," Jack answered with slight anger rising in her voice.

"Yes," Roy took a step closer to her, "you do."

Jack was trying hard to control the anger building up in her. This was a difficult subject for her to discuss, and she usually didn't handle it well. "I'm not interested, Roy." Jack's voice was tight. "Leave it alone."

As Jack purposely turned to get back to her dusting, she heard Roy clear his throat slowly and loudly. Jack listened for the speech that she knew would follow.

"You need to get driving again, Jack. You will never heal the wounds from your past until you face your past. You've got to deal with what happened, Jack."

"My wounds are healed," Jack said angrily from under a chair she was dusting.

"You've been putting band-aids on your wounds for years. They aren't healed, Jack, and you know it."

"I'm fine," she shot back, swallowing her anger. She knew Roy meant well. He always did. Yet this time he had gone too far. He had pushed too much. She was afraid she was getting to the point of saying something that might really hurt the old man, and she didn't want to do that. So with a warning in her voice, she repeated her earlier statement. "I'm fine."

"There you go with 'fine' again." Roy lightened his tone. "I'm old. What if I have a heart attack? You won't be able to get me to the hospital."

"I'll call 911," Jack said quickly, without ever missing a beat.

"Gee, thanks," Roy laughed quietly. "That's kind of you."

"I thought so."

"Jack…" Roy's voice held an unmistakably serious tone, "whether you like it or not, I've arranged driving lessons for you with a very good teacher."

"I thought you were going to teach me." Jack sounded smug.

"Aw, Jack, you're too stubborn for me to teach," Roy teased. "I don't have nearly enough patience!"

Jack laughed, despite the old man's meddling. "And I always thought you had the patience of Job himself."

"I do," Roy smiled confidently at her. "Though I doubt even Job himself could have enough patience for a job like this. That's why I'm bringing in a professional."

"Oh, yeah?" Jack stood up to her full 5'8" stature. "And just who might this professional be?" This conversation had gone on too long and needed to stop right now.

"Matthew Bishop," Roy said quickly. "He's a man of God, with plenty of patience. If he can't teach you, I don't think anyone can!"

Jack's mouth dropped open in shock. "Matthew Bishop?" she sputtered out in disbelief. "You've got to be kidding!"

Roy simply looked at her boldly. "I assure you, My Dear, I'm not kidding in the slightest."

Jack narrowed her eyes at him. She had now entered a full-fledged battle zone and was not about to go down. "I'm not going to go along with this hair-brained idea of yours, Roy," she fumed angrily at him. "No way!"

Roy folded his arms, and merely smiled at Jack victoriously. "Unfortunately, My Dear, you have to. It's all been arranged. And," his gray, bushy eyebrows rose slightly, "your parents have agreed."

Jack felt the sting of the final dart that hit her. If her parents had agreed, then she stood little chance of getting out of it. The fear started enveloping her almost instantly. "Noooo." She sounded like a small, scared child.

"Jack," Roy spoke gently, "it's long overdue. Matthew is the man for the job. Oh," Roy said almost as an afterthought, "you'd better get yourself ready. Matthew will be here in half an hour."

"What!" Jack felt her fear turn to all-out panic. Things were happening too fast. She couldn't get a grip on anything. In a last-ditch effort, Jack said weakly, "I can't go. I have a heavy load of chores today. I can't go."

Just then her father entered Clancy's. He stared at her a minute with a compassionate look. Then he said in a loving voice, "This is your lucky day, Sweetheart. You're being excused from your chores."

Jack slowly walked toward her father as if he were a vision in a dream. Never, in all her life, had her strict, authoritarian father excused her from her chores unless she was sick.

"Father," Jack pleaded in a hollow voice, "please don't make me do this."

"Jack," he replied gently, "it's been almost six years. You need to get behind the wheel again." Placing a loving hand on her shoulder, Max tenderly spoke to his youngest daughter, "I should have made you do it right away." He paused, and then sighed heavily. "I simply didn't have the heart to push you at the time."

Maxwell's eyes clouded over with tears, and Jack instantly turned away from the sight. It was all too much. Complete overload. She couldn't even think of going down that road again.

"Jack," her father squeezed her shoulders reassuringly, "it's past time you learned to conquer this. Matthew is the perfect one to teach you. He's understanding and kind. He'll be patient. You can trust him, Jack. He's a good man."

Jack felt too choked-up to speak. Her father was asking her to face the impossible. All the years of nightmares...the vivid images that replayed in her mind... How could her father ask her to relive that awful time?

As she mechanically climbed the stairs to her room to get ready for her first driving lesson, her heart beat rapidly with fear. Every time she relived it, it was worse. It was always worse in every way. And now she was going to have to relive it with Matthew Bishop. She was now going to have to ride through her worst nightmare with the one man she was trying to avoid. It didn't make any sense. Life could be cruel, but digging up old graves seemed especially cruel. This was one battle that Jack had no idea how to prepare for.

Seven

$\mathscr{A}$s Jack got into the passenger seat of Matthew's black Jeep Cherokee, she felt as though she were running on automatic pilot. The fear in her was so great it made her movements unnatural and mechanical. The harder she tried to get a grip on any part of this situation, the more she saw it slide further away from her. It was like trying to hold water in your hands. The circumstances were quite simply out of her grip, out of her power, and most definitely out of her control.

"I thought we would go up to Sugar Creek State Park," Matthew said sensitively. "There shouldn't be many people there this time of year. There should be plenty of space for you to practice driving."

"Fine," Jack replied in an empty voice that sounded strange even to her own ears. It was almost as if her mind and her voice had a bad connection. Confusion was all her mind was producing. She felt that any jumbled thoughts coming out of her mouth would sound like annoying, perplexing static.

For the next fifteen minutes, as they drove to the park, neither one of them spoke. Yet as Matthew entered the large parking lot, to Jack's surprise, he parked the Jeep and shut off the engine. She turned and stared at him in shock.

He laughed gently, "You didn't think I was going to throw you right behind the wheel, did you?" He laughed again, and Jack felt herself relax a little at the sound.

Matthew then surprised her again by pulling a large bag of chocolate chip cookies from behind his seat and offering one to her. Jack stared a moment at the bag before she shook her head stiffly. She was so nervous that she knew if she ate anything, it would come back up.

Matthew, on the other hand, began chomping contentedly on his first large cookie. He gazed absent-mindedly at the mountain range before them, as if he didn't have a care in the world, but Jack knew him better than that. A sense of sympathy rose in Jack as she felt Matthew was probably just trying to figure out what in the world to do with her. They had once again been thrown together. He probably didn't like these circumstances any more than she did. Jack sat there and watched him eat four cookies before he said a thing.

"It's obvious to me that you're terrified of driving." Matthew's voice was full of compassion. "Maybe it would help if you told me what happened."

"Maybe it wouldn't," Jack answered quickly, as she fidgeted nervously in her seat.

Matthew nodded his head slightly. In the depths of his deep brown eyes she saw the understanding she was longing to see. "Well, in that case," he said gently, as he tossed his cookie bag in the back seat, "I think we should pray."

Panic washed over Jack's features. She was never good at public speaking in any form. She loved to pray, but praying in front of people always made her nervous. She liked Matthew, and normally felt quite comfortable with him. Yet right at the moment, Jack felt too off-balance to attempt to pull off such a feat, even if it was just in front of Matthew.

Matthew read her like a book. "OK," he said in his usual low-key, understanding manner, "I'll pray, and you can listen."

Jack quickly nodded.

Despite her nervousness, she felt Matthew's prayer reach her heart. It was like a soothing ointment to an open wound. She slowly began to feel the chains of her despair releasing her, as a small glimmer of hope shone down upon her. Her heart grabbed at the hope desperately. God was with her. She knew that, but right now she had needed to be reminded of it. The painful memories of the past clung to her tightly. The battle within her raged wildly, and as her hope began to fade, she silently begged God to help her.

As Matthew's prayer ended, Jack knew she had to talk to him. She had to talk to him now, before she lost her courage to do so. "Matthew," urgency filled Jack's voice, "I'm going to try to tell you what happened." Jack hesitated momentarily, and then forced herself to push on. "I need to tell you what happened, but it's not going to be easy, and it may take a little time."

"That's OK, Jack," Matthew reassured her. "Take your time."

As she searched Matthew's kind eyes, she felt drawn to him by the understanding and compassion they held. No one she had ever met before had such a depth of kindness, love, and compassion. He must be what Jesus is like, Jack thought as she closed her eyes tightly for a minute.

"Have I lost you?" The hint of a smile tugged at his lips.

Jack smiled slightly, and then shook her head. "No. No, you haven't lost me. Let's see. I guess I'll start at the beginning."

"That's generally a good place to start," Matthew encouraged her. " I was sixteen and had just received my driver's license. It's every sixteen-year-olds dream. It's your own ticket to freedom. It's a teenager's rite of passage, but for me, it quickly turned into a full-fledged nightmare." Jack paused and blew out a heavy breath. Her eyes were looking ahead of her, at Bear Mountain Range, but they weren't focused on it. Her eyes were seeing the events of that awful winter's night as clearly as if she had been transported back to that time. She clenched her hands tightly into balled fists and pushed on.

"It was a few days before Christmas and my family had gone to the theater to see the Nutcracker. I was home, stuck in bed with the flu. Then the phone started ringing." Jack paused and closed her eyes. "I can still hear the phone ringing. Six years later, I can still hear that blasted phone ringing. Sometimes...oftentimes when I think about this, I wonder if the phone will ever stop ringing in my mind."

Jack opened her eyes and quickly glanced at Matthew, only to find a kindhearted face looking back at her. He had such a special way of sending love and support through his caring eyes. Jack felt embraced by him and felt the courage to persevere.

As she once again focused in on that night long ago and tried to continue the story, she found she couldn't. Tears were rising within her and began to spill out rapidly. Matthew simply took her hand and held it gently within his own.

"I'm sorry," Jack squeaked out in a tight voice.

Matthew squeezed her hand reassuringly. "Don't apologize for being the victim of life's garbage." He paused and cleared his throat. "I'd really like to help you through this. Please let me." Silently he prayed that she would.

Jack nodded, grateful for his understanding, and persisted. "I stumbled out of bed and grabbed the ringing phone. It was Mallard's, the bar down by the south lake docks. The bartender said my grandfather was down there drinking himself into oblivion. He told me someone should come out and get him before he drank himself to death."

Jack sighed again, as she wrung her fingers in frustration. Relaying this story was a gut-wrenching experience for her. "Before you think of my grandfather as an awful person, I need to fill you in on his background a little." Jack looked at Matthew, and he nodded seriously.

"You see," Jack continued in a heavy voice, "Grandpa was a strong Christian man. When my grandmother lost her battle with cancer ten years ago, Grandpa began to crumble on the outside as well as the inside. She died around Christmas, and every Christmas after that was an intense struggle...I mean an all-out battle for him to get through. He always felt guilty that Grandma died. He felt that if his faith were stronger, she'd be alive today."

"That's not true," Matthew became adamant. "Losing his wife had nothing to do with his faith. God's ways are different than our ways and don't always make sense to us."

Jack searched his face intently. "I know that," the forced words came out in a grieved whisper, "but no one could ever seem to get that through Grandpa's head. He went to his grave believing it was all somehow his fault."

"That's such a tragedy." Sorrow filled Matthew's voice.

Jack nodded in agreement, and then looked away. "Shortly after Grandma's death he turned to drinking." Her voice had become trance-like. "Especially at Christmastime." Jack paused thoughtfully, and then said sadly, "I think he did want to drink himself into oblivion. I think he really wanted to die. He could never seem to escape the pain of losing her."

"Jack…" Matthew's voice was tight and emotion-filled, "I'm so sorry." He paused and put a hand on her shoulder. "Please don't think I'm here to judge you, or your grandfather. I simply want to help."

Jack nodded again and pushed on. "I drove down to Mallard's to pick him up. I hated that place. It was loud, smoky, and filled with a lot of tough-looking guys. Oftentimes men were passed out right at the bar." Jack closed her eyes, trying to rid her mind of that awful scene, but the images stayed vivid, refusing to fade.

"When you walked into the room," Jack's voice was small and her eyes were still closed, "the smell of liquor, smoke, sweat, urine, and vomit just overwhelmed you." Jack opened her eyes, and looked directly at Matthew for a second. "I remember praying that I wouldn't pass out or vomit before I got my grandfather out of that place. I was so scared for both of us."

Jack put a hand over her eyes, trying to shut the memory out. "The bartender helped me drag my grandfather to the car. He dumped him in the passenger seat and walked away without saying a thing." Jack took her hand away from her face and blew out a loud breath. "But I'll never forget his eyes. The bartender's eyes were narrow, almost beady. They reminded me so much of a rat. I hated him at that moment. I hated him for serving my grandfather long after he should have stopped. It's like he handed a drowning man a ton of concrete." Jack turned, and looked again at Matthew. "It took me along time to forgive that bartender. I hated him for so long."

"It's a normal feeling for what you went through," Matthew's voice showed his concern.

Jack simply nodded. "Some time later I came to accept the fact that if Mallard's hadn't served

Grandpa the liquor, he would have gone someplace that would have. Grandpa was dead set on getting as drunk as he could."

Matthew nodded sympathetically.

"The ride home was awful," Jack balled her hands into fists again. "Grandpa was drunk as a skunk, and his temper and stubbornness were at an all-time high. He argued with me about everything." The anguish in Jack's voice tore through Matthew's heart like a knife. "And, the thing about arguing with a drunk is that you'll never win. There is no way they can see any kind of reason in the stupor they're in."

"That's true," Matthew agreed as he studied Jack closely. He felt so ripped up inside. He wasn't sure how much she could take. He wanted to stop Jack from reliving this incident again, yet at the same time, he felt she needed to talk about it. He silently prayed for wisdom from above.

"Grandpa was arguing with me for taking him away from the bar. He kept telling me he could handle it, and that it was none of my business what he did with his life."

"What did you say?"

"Nothing," Jack's voice had gone completely flat. "Absolutely nothing. You can't reason with a drunk. Grandpa had taught me that lesson from past experience. And," Jack exhaled and closed her eyes for a moment, "a mean drunk is even worse."

Jack opened her eyes and continued in a quiet tone. "I just let him blow off steam while I tried to concentrate on the road. It was wintertime in Maine and the roads were icy. There was black ice, and you just couldn't see it. By the time I knew we'd hit the ice, the car was spinning, sliding, or swerving. It wasn't fun."

"It sounds like a nightmare," Matthew said in a protective tone.

"Yes," Jack stared out her window at the mountains. "Combine the road conditions with a very drunk, angry passenger, and a brand-new sixteen-year-old driver. It was an awful nightmare…but it was about to get worse."

"Every time I hit ice, Grandpa would try to grab the steering wheel. He'd try to take over the driving from the passenger seat, and we'd be swerving all over the road. He kept shouting at me that I was going to get us both killed."

"So," the frustration was building in Matthew's voice, "you were not only battling icy road conditions, but you were also battling a drunk who wanted to take over the driving."

"Yes," Jack admitted regretfully. "Grandpa was a big man. He stood 6'4" and weighed around two hundred and fifty pounds. When he made a grab at me, or shoved me, it really threw me."

"I can imagine," Matthew said heatedly.

"We had just about made it home." Jack's voice hung heavy with disappointment. I was hopeful everything was going to work out, but when we turned on to East Shore Road, things got nasty again. You know the hairpin turn about half way down the road?" Jack asked as she glanced at Matthew.

Matthew nodded, imagining what had happened.

"Well," Jack's voice had grown so tight, she could barely force her words out, "we never made it through that turn." Jack exhaled loudly. She was determined to finish. She'd made it this far. She didn't want to have to go through this again at another time, yet the images were there. She could see the awful images as clearly as if she were watching a movie. She clenched her fists so tightly that her hands hurt.

"We never made it through…" she repeated in a small voice. "We hit ice again and Grandpa grabbed for the wheel and this time he got it. He swung the wheel sharply to the right. I was trying so hard to break his ironclad grip on the wheel — but I couldn't. I wasn't strong enough. Even when

Grandpa was drunk, he was still as strong as a bear. He drove us right into a huge pine tree."

Tears were rolling down Jack's face. She continued to stare ahead in a trance. Matthew reached out and gently took her hand, but she didn't feel it. Her mind was too focused on the accident.

"There was so much blood everywhere," Jack stated in a voice that was still enveloped in disbelief. "Everywhere," she said again. "The dashboard, the seats, the steering wheel we had been fighting over…yet worst of all, it was all over me and Grandpa. It was all over my face, in my eyes and in my mouth, too."

Jack paused a moment, and as she turned toward Matthew, she wiped her face with her shirtsleeve. "I will never forget the taste of blood in my mouth. Isn't it strange that when I tell this story I can still taste blood in my mouth? Even after all these years?"

Matthew nodded, clearly shaken. Jack turned her gaze back toward the mountains. They offered no comfort, yet they were a needed diversion from the anguish she saw in Matthew's face.

"Another thing about the accident that I remember clearly is the sound of someone screaming. It was a loud, scared, painful cry, and it didn't seem to stop. It filled the night air in a lingering, haunting way." Jack wiped her eyes, and turned to ward Matthew. "I'll never forget the sound."

Matthew eyes were filled with tears, and his voice too choked up to speak. He looked as defeated as Jack felt. He simply took Jack's hand and squeezed it in a reassuring way, hoping she would feel his love and support. As he let go of her hand, he watched her carefully. His concern for her was great. The burden she had been carrying around all these years was too big. It was crushing and suffocating, and he didn't know how she carried it.

Jack continued in a small, far-away voice. "I still recall how confused I felt when I recognized the screaming as my own voice. It was so weird. I felt so disconnected from my body; yet at the same time, acutely aware of the situation I was in. What a strange experience."

Jack paused and breathed deeply. She slowly flexed her fingers back and forth. She had been squeezing them so tightly they ached.

Again, in a matter-of-fact tone, she pushed on. "I'm not exactly sure how long it was until my father found us. I had passed out several times. My father, mother, and sisters found us when they returned from the theater." Jack blew out a forced breath. "They said that my grandfather had died upon impact. He wasn't wearing a seatbelt and flew into the windshield when we hit the tree."

"I'm so sorry, Jack," Matthew put a caring hand on her shoulder. He felt so helpless. He wanted to take her pain away and erase the awful memories. A hopeless feeling washed over him as he knew he couldn't. He prayed desperately that God would.

"So am I." Jack shook her head slowly. "I ended up in the hospital for a week with a concussion, broken ribs, and a broken arm. Grandpa, on the other hand, never knew what hit him."

Tears again were rolling down Jack's face in torrents. In a choked-up voice she said, "I miss him so much. He was a different man before Grandma died. We were so close. Everyone loved Grandpa Miller."

Jack turned and glared out the window angrily. "To this day, the whole thing angers me. His alcoholism, the struggles we went through, the accident…"Jack was rambling at a quick pace, "and that my last words with a grandfather that I loved so dearly were argumentative. I just hate the whole thing."

Jack slowly turned and looked at Matthew. Her features were covered in anguish and defeat. "I loved him so much. I think I will always question my judgments that night, and whether or not I made the right choices. I have to live with the results of my decisions, and it's not an easy thing."

"Jack," Matthew spoke tenderly as he gathered the hurting young woman into his arms. She seemed no more than a broken, helpless, lost child.

He held her tightly, rocking her gently in his arms as he listened to her heart-wrenching sobs. The sound shook him to his very core.

"Oh, Dear God," Matthew prayed heavy-heartedly, "heal Jack. Help her give this burden to You. This is much too great for anyone to carry. Heal her, Father. Touch her heart and heal her. And please," Matthew added in a helpless tone, "please direct me as to how I can help her. Give me the words…help me to show her that I really care."

As the tears subsided, Jack reluctantly pulled away from the comfort of Matthew's arms. "Matthew, one reason that I opened up to you so honestly is that I wanted you to understand completely why I don't want to drive again." Jack paused, and then managed to say in a stronger voice filled with a greater determination, "I won't drive again, Matthew. You need to understand that."

The only thing that the young pastor understood was that a young woman had been through an awful ordeal. The scars she carried with her were not only deep, they were still painful and raw.

"I think this has been enough for today, Jack." Matthew spoke softly to the young woman next to him. She nodded and he started up the Jeep and slowly headed back toward the Inn.

"I won't drive again, Matthew," Jack vowed with growing conviction in her tone.

Matthew didn't respond. He knew this was no time for logic. He merely nodded at her and took her hand and held it gently within his own. It was the only thing he could think to do at the moment to convey his concern for her.

As they pulled into the circular drive of the Inn, they could see Ethan, Nicholas, and Flyer down by the beach. "Would you like to walk a bit?" Matthew asked her sensitively.

Jack nodded. "You should get to know Ethan and Nicholas better. You'd like them."

As Matthew and Jack made their way over to the sandy beach, Jack gasped at the sight in front of her. Flyer was licking chocolate ice cream off of young Nicholas's pudgy little face. Jack ran to the blonde two-year-old and scooped him up in her arms.

"Ethan!" she scolded her brother-in-law, "That is completely disgusting! I can't believe you'd let Flyer lick Nicholas on his face like this."

"I thought it was kind of cute," Ethan shrugged his broad shoulder sheepishly.

"Do you know what else Flyer licks with that tongue of his? It's gross!"

"I hadn't thought of that," Ethan confessed quietly.

"Andy would have your head."

"Well, let's not tell her," Ethan smiled sheepishly at Matthew in a conspiratorial way. "What she doesn't know is not going to hurt her."

Jack glared at Ethan for a moment. "I'm going to wash the dog germs and slobber off Nicholas's face." With that, she marched off toward the Inn.

Ethan looked over at Matthew, and they smiled at each other. "I guess I still have a lot to learn as a Dad."

Matthew just laughed. "My Mom used to say it amazed her that any of us reached our eighteenth birthdays."

Ethan smiled and nodded. "How did the driving lesson go?"

"I think remarkably well," Matthew answered thoughtfully.

"You actually got Jack behind the wheel?" Ethan asked in disbelief.

Matthew shook his head solemnly. "Another time. Today we just talked." Matthew sighed heavily. "She told me all about the accident."

"Really?" Ethan was clearly shocked. "There are not many that she confided in about that."

"I know she told her parents and her sisters," Matthew squeezed the back of his aching neck. "I would guess she's probably told Bradley, too."

"I don't think so," Ethan was quick to reply.

"Really?" Matthew looked at Ethan feeling confused. "She's supposed to be marrying him. You think she'd trust him enough."

"That's the way it's supposed to work." Ethan's words were heavy and frustrated. He dug his hands deep into his pockets before continuing. "Jack's relationship with Bradley Clarke is very complex."

"I've noticed," Matthew commented, feeling frustrated himself.

"You want to know what I think?" Ethan raised his eyebrows slightly.

"Yes," Matthew looked at the tall man interestedly.

"I think she's marrying Bradley Clarke because of some sort of promise she made to her Grandpa Miller."

Matthew's face dropped. "Oh…"

"Yes," Ethan nodded firmly. "Jack loved Grandpa Miller dearly. They were always very close. Grandpa Miller loved Bradley Clarke like a son, though I'm really not sure why." Ethan paused a minute to adjust the Red Sox baseball cap on his head.

"Grandpa Miller always told Jack from an early age how perfect she and Bradley would be together. He told Jack many times that he believed God brought her and Bradley together for a very special purpose." Ethan exhaled loudly. "I think Jack feels trapped in the relationship. I think she resigned herself to a marriage with Bradley out of some sort of guilt she feels about losing Grandpa Miller." Ethan shook his head disgustedly. "They don't even have much in common."

"Sounds like you don't like Bradley very much." Matthew studied Ethan carefully.

Ethan laughed. "It won't take you long to find out that no one really likes Bradley Clarke. He's full of himself, and only thinks of himself." Ethan looked at Matthew and shook his head slowly. "I don't mean to sound harsh, but it's the sad truth. You'll find it out soon enough. Oh, when do you start their marriage counseling sessions?"

"This Saturday," Matthew replied matter-of-factly.

"Well," Ethan said seriously, "I'll be praying for you. It's not going to be easy for you."

"Somehow, I already knew that." Matthew sadly nodded and then gazed out across Eagle Lake. "I think it's going to be one of the toughest things I've ever done."

Ethan nodded sympathetically. "Like I said before, I'll be praying for you."

"Thanks."

Ethan shook his head sadly. "Don't thank me, Matthew. You're going to need it."

Eight

As Jack was sailing toward the village of Sugar Creek, she anxiously watched her two mountain dogs. Flyer was curled up as though he were about to take a nap. Docker, on the other hand, looked as though he absolutely, positively regretted his decision to get on board Jack's catamaran. Jack had bribed Docker with a handful of peanut butter dog cookies. Now that the cookies were gone, the old dog paced around nervously, looking for any escape off the boat.

"It's all right, Boy." Jack's tone was soothing as she patted the worried dog. "I promise not to dump you this time. We'll take a nice, slow ride. You'll see."

Docker stared at Jack as skeptically as a dog possibly could. He didn't believe her promise, nor would he be comforted by her soothing words. He knew he had been tricked, and Jack felt mildly guilty for it. Docker didn't like her boat, and right at the moment, Jack was pretty sure he didn't like her.

Jack continued to pat Docker absent-mindedly as she thought about her task at hand. Today was the first marriage counseling session she and

Bradley would have with Matthew. Her mind was racing on overdrive, and her heart was full of worry. She knew that she should relax and trust in God for all things, yet she found that when the rubber met the road and she was going through a difficult time, she was just so much better at worrying than trusting. She wasn't proud of this fact, yet unfortunately it was true. As she reached over and patted Flyer, she tossed a quick prayer to heaven asking for God's blessing on the meeting today.

When Jack reached the North Shore, she carefully maneuvered her cat over to the town docks. She spotted Matthew immediately, and they waved to each other. He was in front of Sundae School, the ice cream shop where they all agreed to meet.

As she was about to dock her cat, the owner of the ice cream shop spotted her and walked onto the docks to tease her. "Hey, Jack Miller," Hank yelled out in a hassling tone, pretending to be annoyed and angry, "would you mind moving that piece of floating garbage away from my store. It's bad for my business. It's going to chase away my paying customers!"

Jack smiled at him and laughed as she threw a dock line out to Matthew. It was always the same routine with old Hank Webber. He had been teasing Jack about her boat since she was a young girl.

"Good to see you, Hank," Jack said in a friendly tone. "Has the summer tourism started up for you yet?"

Hank let out a loud laugh. "My dear child, it's not likely to start any time soon if that barge of yours stays in front of my store. It's so ugly that it will drive away my customers."

Matthew and Jack laughed at him. Hank could be grumpy and ornery at times, yet underneath his tough skin, he had a heart of gold. He would do just about anything for anyone...but he never wanted anyone to know about his good deeds. He felt it might ruin his cranky reputation.

As soon as Jack landed, Docker jumped off the boat, followed directly by Flyer. They ran over to Matthew, with both tails wagging, and half their bodies wiggling from excitement. Matthew did not disappoint the enthusiastic dogs. He scratched behind their ears, patted their heads, and rubbed their furry bellies. They were in dog heaven.

Old Hank turned to Jack with an especially irritable expression on his face. "Your dogs are totally shameless. Look at the way those mutts have taken over my dock." He shook his head as he watched the dogs closely. "Shameless."

Then he turned to Matthew and said in a cantankerous-sounding manner, "Are you just going to hang out on my dock and chase away all my customers?" He threw his hands on his hips and leaned closer to Matthew and said, "This here dock is for paying customers only. If you don't plan on buying something, then take your mutts and beat it."

"I warned you," Jack said playfully to Matthew as she laughed at old Hank. "He's the type of man that tests your patience."

Hank scowled at Jack, and then glanced back toward Matthew.

"Actually," Matthew's tone was laid-back, "I thought we might be brave enough to try some of that ice cream of yours."

"You're going to have to buy it." Hank's stance was challenging. "If I stood around the docks all day and handed out my ice cream for free, I'd be out of business in no time."

"I've brought my wallet." Matthew couldn't help but laugh. Old Hank was quite a character.

"Good thing. You'll need it." With that said, Hank turned on his heal and walked into his shop.

"Since this is our first marriage counseling session," Matthew got up from where he had been patting the dogs, "I thought I'd treat you and Bradley to ice cream."

"That sounds like a great idea," Jack eyed the ice cream shop excitedly. "Why don't we just go in and look around while we're waiting for Bradley to come?"

As they browsed Hank's assortment of flavors, Jack asked Matthew what his favorite flavor was.

"I don't have a favorite flavor," Matthew laughed lightly. "As long as it's ice cream, I'll love it." He paused in front of the Triple Chocolate Explosion and studied the container carefully. "What are you going to have?"

"Vanilla," Jack answered as she studied a new flavor that Hank had invented. Hank was always mixing up new flavors. Most of the time they were very good.

"Toppings?" Matthew asked, as he moved on to look at Hank's Four-Cookie Collision.

"None."

Matthew whipped his head away from the counter and stared at Jack. "All you want is vanilla ice cream, with no toppings?"

"That's what I like." Jack glanced over at him with a curious expression.

"You know," Matthew sounded slightly insulted, "just because I'm a poor country pastor on a low salary doesn't mean I can't afford anything more than plain, old vanilla ice cream. And," Matthew took a step closer to her, "for the record, I can afford toppings, too."

Before Jack could answer, Bradley appeared from the back of the store, howling with laughter. "It's nothing personal against you, Pastor. Jacilyn has been ordering plain, old vanilla ice cream for years."

Matthew looked at Jack and then raised his eyebrows questioningly. "For years, huh?"

Jack nodded, clearly amused by the conversation. "I occasionally get some Mud on it, but most of the time I like it just plain."

Matthew's mouth swung open in shock. "Why that's completely disgusting. I believe you Maine people are a little too earthy for me."

Everyone within earshot of the conversation broke up laughing. "Pastor," Bradley gasped between fits of laughter, "you are so funny. I'm going to have to stop by your church one of these Sundays. You must be a total crackup from the pulpit."

Matthew stared at Bradley a second before answering. Jack sensed he was trying to figure him out. "I hope you do stop by the church sometime, still what you Maine people do to your ice cream should be against the law." Matthew turned and looked over at Hank. "There are limits on creativity, Hank. New flavors I understand. Mud I don't."

Once again everyone laughed. Jack put a hand on Matthew's arm, trying to explain what Mud was all about. "Hank invented a chocolate sauce called Hank's Maine Mud. It's sold all around the country in gourmet shops."

Matthew's face dropped. "Really?"

Jack nodded and began to laugh again.

"Well, that definitely sounds much better than what I was picturing. I thought he was digging up his backyard."

After the three of them got their ice cream, they went out to sit at the white umbrella-tables on the dock. "So," Matthew began as he dug into his ice cream excitedly, "when is the actual date for you two?"

Jack suddenly felt very uncomfortable. Any time the conversation turned to the upcoming wedding, she felt nervous and uneasy and just plain awkward.

"Labor Day weekend," Bradley replied confidently.

Flyer and Docker came up to Jack, and she dumped some of her ice cream onto the dock for them. She was suddenly losing her appetite. Her stomach was turning into knots.

After Matthew opened up the session in prayer, Bradley hit him with a curve ball. "Pastor, I need to level with you on something."

"Shoot," Matthew eyed Bradley intently.

"You know that I'm studying to be a pastor."

"Yes, I do."

"Actually," Bradley admitted proudly, "I'll be graduated by our wedding date."

"I'm aware of that," Jack noticed Matthew's apprehension immediately.

Bradley sounded like a politician building a case. By this time both Jack and Matthew were eyeing him suspiciously.

"Well, to be honest with you, Pastor," Bradley stated in a patronizing tone, "I simply don't have time for these little meetings of yours. I mean, well, quite frankly, with all the papers I have to write between now and graduation, I can't see myself going through these sessions."

Jack drew a breath in sharply. Bradley was not only being arrogant, he was being downright rude. Jack turned to Matthew to see how he would respond to this.

Matthew stared at Bradley hard for a moment. Jack could only imagine what was going through his head. "Well, Bradley," Matthew's tone was less-than-friendly-sounding, "let me be honest with you. Every couple that I marry must go through this marriage counseling. I don't care if you're training to be the President of the United States. You must complete the course."

Matthew and Bradley eyed each other for several seconds. Jack thought they looked like two bulls about ready to butt heads. She found herself nervously gripping her fingers as she watched them.

"On the other hand," Matthew continued slowly, as he kept steady eye contact with Bradley, "there are several other options here. You can move the wedding date back. You can graduate a semester later. Or," he added indifferently, "you can have another pastor marry you."

"That may be our answer here." Bradley jumped all over the third option. "Nothing personal, Pastor Bishop, but I think that may work best for me."

The silence that was forming was broken by one word from Jack. In a low, quiet voice she stated adamantly, "No."

"What did you say?" Bradley asked, turning to her in shock.

"I said, 'No.'" Jack was growing angrier by the second. She felt like knocking Bradley off the dock. "He is the pastor of my church, and I want him to marry us."

Bradley stared at Jack seriously for a minute, before letting out a loud laugh. "Jacilyn, we're going to have to work on this submission thing."

"On you being submissive?" Jack challenged.

Bradley laughed nervously. "As you can see for yourself, Pastor, I've got myself a live wire here."

No one laughed at his attempt to cover up his poor manners. "Well listen, Jacilyn," Bradley turned in his seat to face her directly, "I'm going to have to run. I'm swamped with schoolwork. You work this out with the good pastor, and let me know how the cards fall." With that said, Bradley rose, kissed Jack on the cheek, and left.

Jack glanced nervously in Matthew's direction for a moment and then turned her full attention to her dogs. As she patted each one, she said in an embarrassed voice, "I'm so sorry, Matthew. He was more than rude, and I can't honestly think of a thing to say in his defense."

"That's good, Jack. When someone is as rude as Bradley has been, you shouldn't think of excuses for them." It was one of the first times that Jack could ever remember Matthew's voice being absolutely irritated.

"You're right," Jack said, feeling ashamed of how Bradley had acted. "I'm sorry we wasted your time."

"Maybe it won't be a waste of time after all," Matthew said in a lighter voice. "Why don't you tell me what you like about Bradley? I think it would be good for me, right about now, to hear about some of his finer points."

"I'm all rattled," Jack said anxiously. "I can't seem to think."

"Would you like to go for a walk around town?" Matthew asked easily.

"That sounds wonderful." Jack felt relieved at being rescued from having to explain anything further about her fiancé.

As they started to walk, Docker and Flyer got up and padded along behind them. The main wharf was full of all kinds of interesting shops. There were restaurants that offered full course meals, bakeries, cookie specialty shops, gourmet candy shops, fudge shops, antique shops, boating stores, clothing stores, fishing nooks, and much more. All of the best stores in Sugar Creek were located right on the main wharf.

As they walked on the cobblestone streets, they soon came upon Aunt Diana's Fudge Shop. Matthew stopped abruptly and turned to Jack. "Do you like fudge?" he asked her with the excitement of a child.

"I love it." Jack was finally being to feel herself relax after the earlier incident with Bradley.

"Well, then," Matthew opened up the red door to the shop, "we should definitely explore this place."

Aunt Diana was a fun-loving, friendly woman in her early forties. She was involved in more charitable organizations in Sugar Creek than anyone else Jack knew. She also knew how to make fudge better than anyone else. Jack was carried away with the smell as soon as she entered the shop.

"Matthew, Jack," Diana greeted her customers with her usual warmth, "how nice of you to stop by." Jack always marveled at how Diana could make you feel that you were doing her a favor by stopping by her shop.

"It smells great in here!" Matthew exclaimed enthusiastically, as he eyed her fudge counter like a wolf eyeing a sheep pack.

"That's always good to hear," Diana smiled at them. "I've just made a fresh batch of chocolate-peanut butter. Would you like to try some?"

Both Matthew and Jack nodded eagerly.

"This is great!" The chocolate and peanut butter combination started melting immediately in Jack's mouth. "You make the smoothest, most delicious fudge I've ever tasted."

"If you ever have a part-time job open for a taster, let me know." Matthew quickly helped himself to another piece of soft fudge. He looked like he was in paradise.

Diana laughed at them. "I'm glad you're enjoying this. It's always nice to have good reviews!"

Before they left the fudge shop, Matthew bought a pound of the still-warm chocolate-peanut butter fudge. They walked around the quaint town sharing the fudge and enjoying each other's company. Before they knew it, they were at the town green. The dogs enjoyed running and playing and having free rein in the nearly empty park.

"So," Matthew smiled playfully at Jack, "was it like your heart just connected with Bradley's heart? Did you fall madly in love with him, and know beyond a shadow of a doubt that God made you for each other?"

Jack laughed loudly. "Don't be ridiculous!" She snagged another piece of fudge from his bag. "That type of stuff only happens in movies!"

Matthew stopped walking, looked at Jack directly, and raised his brown eyebrows at her. As he sat down on the thick, green grass, he continued to stare at Jack questioningly.

It didn't take long for Jack to realize what she had said, or the trap she had fallen into. "Oh, well…of course," she stuttered, as she dropped to the lawn beside Matthew. "That's the way it was with Bradley and me." As Matthew's look grew intense, Jack rambled on. "Just that way. That's exactly how it was. That way."

Matthew nibbled on his fudge for a minute before saying anything. "I certainly hope so, Jack," his quiet voice was filled with conviction. "Because if you're not head over heels in love with each other, and committed to this marriage three hundred percent, it probably will never last."

Jack stared at Matthew unsure of what to say. She knew that lying was wrong. And lying to a man of God had to be really, really wrong. It almost seemed twice as bad. Jack bit her lower lip, not knowing what to say next.

"This is a tough world we live in," Matthew went on slowly, letting Jack off the hook for the moment. He scanned the park thoughtfully and then returned to her. He held her eyes with his own and then spoke slowly, yet almost urgently, from his heart. "In any marriage, you're going to face tough times. You'll both make mistakes. There may be times when one or both of you will want to walk away from it. You'll need a deep love and commitment that's rooted in Christ."

Matthew paused, looked at the ground for a minute, and then studied Jack more intently. "Jack, you've got to be honest here. You've got to know in your heart that if you don't walk down the aisle with Bradley, you'll regret it the rest of your life. You've got to know in your heart," Matthew said, touching her shoulder gently, "that he's the only one for you."

Jack felt so choked up that she couldn't speak. How could she tell Matthew that she felt it would be the biggest mistake of her life marrying Bradley? She didn't want to walk down the aisle with him. She knew in her heart he wasn't the one for her. On top of it all, how could she break a promise to her grandpa that she'd marry this man, even if she didn't love him? Her eyes began to tear up, and she bit her lip to keep from bawling.

"Jack," Matthew whispered compassionately as he reached for her hand, "if he isn't the one for you, don't go through with it. It's not too late to walk away.

God's man for you is one who loves you with all his heart, and will cherish you for the rest of his life."

Jack was staring at Matthew. She knew she was staring at him, yet she couldn't seem to help it. She was looking at him as though she had just received her sight. She felt drawn to him like a magnet. She couldn't tear her eyes away from his. She felt her-self being drawn in deeper and deeper.

He was staring at her, too. Gazing at her with such love and open admiration that she knew, for the first time in her life, what it was like to be truly loved by a man. Loved for herself, not loved for what others thought she was or could do. Matthew knew her well. He knew her better than most, and he loved her. What a wonderful feeling.

Jack smiled at him, and he smiled back. She felt completely lost in his eyes. As though someone were pushing them together, their faces came clos-er and closer. Feelings Jack had never experienced before were growing within her at a furious pace. Passion, excitement, and obsession raced through her. A deep burning desire to be close, and a long-ing to touch exploded within both of them. An inch before their lips were to meet, Flyer came racing up, with Docker right behind, and pounced on Matthew and his bag of fudge. The bag of fudge flew in the air, and the dogs followed it like a mis-sile to a target. Matthew landed with a thud on his back. Instantly his hands covered his face. He lay there for several minutes before Jack gained the courage to speak.

"Are you OK?" she asked in a wobbly voice, still feeling very much confused and dazed by what had almost happened.

With his hands still covering his face, Matthew replied in a husky, choked-up voice, "No, Jack. I am definitely not OK."

He took his hands away from his face, and as he sat up, he looked at Jack closely. In a pointed voice, he asked, "How are you?"

"Not great," Jack admitted numbly.

They sat there for several minutes in silence. Matthew stood up and began brushing the grass, dog hair, and crumbs of fudge off himself. When he had finished, he ran a nervous hand through his hair, and sighed loudly.

"Jack," he stated uneasily, "considering what just almost happened here..." He paused and ran his hand through his hair again. "I mean, under the present circumstances...I actually think Bradley is right."

"Right?" Jack was even more confused than she was a minute before. "Bradley? Right?" Jack shook her head trying to clear away the cobwebs. This entire situation didn't make sense. Nothing did at the moment. "What do you mean?"

"I mean," Matthew exhaled loudly, "that Bradley suggested getting another pastor to marry you two." Matthew paused and looked Jack in the eye, "Considering everything…I think that's a good idea."

Jack knew she was going to cry, and she also knew that there was going to be nothing she could do to stop herself. Tears were inevitable. She felt them stinging at the corners of her eyes, and then start to roll down her face.

Matthew knelt down, and held the sides of Jack's face in his hands. He turned her face gently up toward his. When she looked at him, he slowly let his hands down. "Jack," his voice was loving, "I'm so sorry. I can't marry you and Bradley," Matthew sighed deeply. "If I were you, I'd pray long and hard about that union. I don't believe it's God's will. I've had doubts about you two since we first met."

Jack turned away and wiped her tears on the sleeve of her cotton jacket. More tears replaced the ones she wiped away. She knew it was useless. The tears seemed to be flowing out of her in torrents.

"Jack, please don't marry Bradley out of a promise you made to your grandpa." The urgency in Matthew's voice made her look at him. "The only reason you should marry someone is that he is God's perfect choice for you." A sad smile spread across his face. "When that right choice comes along, you'll know it," Matthew said in a tight voice, as he blinked back tears of his own. "You'll find yourself head over heels in love. You won't find yourself trying so hard to love someone. It will just come naturally. You'll find yourself thinking about him all the time. You won't want a day to go by without talking to him and hearing the sound of his voice. You'll know, Jack." Matthew's voice had grown husky, "You'll know God's choice for you. Don't settle for anything less."

As Jack watched Matthew slowly get up and walk away, she thought she was going to be sick. She did know God's choice for her. She was watching him walk out her life, as she prepared to spend her life with a man she definitely didn't love and quite possibly didn't even like.

There had been so many times that she wished she could cancel the wedding with Bradley. Every time she thought seriously about doing so, the thoughts of her grandpa and the promise she made to him made her feel overwhelmingly guilty. He had died with her at the wheel. Didn't she owe it to him to fulfill this wish? It was the one thing that Jack knew Grandpa wanted her to do, so to honor him she would do it. She also knew that it would be settling for less than God's choice for her. It would be the biggest and most painful compromise she'd ever have to make in her life.

Nine

$\mathcal{J}$ack sailed home in a daze. Somehow she managed to dock her boat and slip away from the crowd at the Inn to one of her favorite hiding places. Except for the beach area, the Inn's shoreline was surrounded by large, gray rocks and heavily decorated with pine trees and evergreen trees. Just south of the boathouse, there was an area well hidden by thick, evergreen trees. Only the Millers knew the path to this spot, and they kept it as a family secret. Here among the rocks, water, and evergreens, you were guaranteed a quiet, private place to think.

Sitting on a large, flat rock, Jack hugged Flyer and Docker tightly. The tears rolled down her face like a river. The heartache she was feeling inside was nothing like any feeling she had ever known before. Pain. Pain so sharp and deep that she didn't think that an actual knife in her heart would have hurt more.

As she sat on the rock, she could hear the sounds of the lake. People were laughing and playing in the water. Motorboats with big, loud engines would pass by quickly. The fishing boats would pass by more slowly, as their smaller engines made a dull putting noise against the water. Sailboats would pass by her quietly, with only the sound of the wind tugging on the sails as the boats glided across the water in a graceful manner.

Everyone around her was so alive, so free. Jack shook her head at the irony of the situation. The lake around her sounded so alive, and she had never felt more dead in her life. It was as though the life had been drained right out of her. The only feeling she did have was an acute sense of emptiness and loss. It was as though hollowness was ringing throughout her. It was an awful feeling that she could not seem to make go away.

As she watched the sun setting across the lake, the world around her became lit in a golden glow. As the sun's rays said goodnight to the world, they danced on the water before her, creating a heavenly-looking, golden path before her. Jack felt stunned to see such beauty, while feeling so dead inside. How strange and ironic, she thought sadly. It just didn't make sense that such beauty and heartache could coexist.

Half an hour later, she sat in the pitch dark. The sounds of the lake still surrounded her, but they were gentle, quiet sounds of the night. The lapping of the water against the land as the two met; the quieter, hushed voices of people, and the lull of an occasional passing boat were all familiar, comforting sounds to Jack.

She didn't know how long she sat there, surrounded by the silence, before she noticed the beams from the flashlights coming her way. The dogs saw them, too, and their heads rose in curiosity.

"Jack, are you down there?" Sam's anxious voice called to her.

"Yeah, Sam," she answered in a heavy voice. "I'm here with Flyer and Docker."

She could hear Sam's voice talking in a hushed whisper. Soon all her sisters were around her.

"What happened?" Andy asked her gently, as she climbed up on the rock to sit down next to her. "Didn't you have your first counseling session with Matthew today?"

Jack nodded her head slowly. "Yes."

"I guess it didn't go very well," Jay remarked as she laid some logs in the small stone fireplace below her.

"No," Jack answered in a hoarse voice. "It didn't go very well."

Jack could hear her sisters sigh heavily as she absent-mindedly watched Jay start the small campfire. The blaze was not only inviting, but warming as well. Jack stretched her fingers toward the blaze, enjoying its heat.

"Did Bradley act like his usual self?" Jay asked accusingly.

"I guess you could say that," Jack mumbled, as she stared at the flames dancing before her. She sighed loudly, and then pushed on. "He basically told Matthew that he didn't have time for marriage counseling."

Jack could hear Sam's sharp intake of breath. "How did Matthew react to that?"

Jack actually laughed a little. "As you can imagine, not very well. He told Bradley that if he couldn't make time for the counseling sessions, he could find himself another pastor to marry us."

Andy was sitting next to Jack and put an arm lovingly around her. "I'm so sorry, Hon. It sounds like you had a rough time. You don't need to say anything more if you don't want to, but," she squeezed her shoulders, "if you want to talk, we're here for you."

"It only gets worse." Jack shook her head.

"Somehow that doesn't surprise me," Jay noted sarcastically. "I'll bet Bradley didn't take Matthew's news well."

"Actually," Jack said in a matter-of-fact tone, "he didn't take it all that badly. He was more than fine with getting another pastor."

"Really?" all three sisters said in unison.

Jack laughed and nodded. "Yes. I was the one who had trouble with it. I was adamant about Matthew marrying us because he is my pastor."

"So how was it left?" Andy asked seriously.

"Bradley basically told me to handle things, and then he left. He just walked out of the meeting."

"You're kidding?" Sam asked in disbelief.

"I'm not surprised," Jay's words flew out angrily. "Bradley is a jerk, and he acted like a jerk. I really don't know why that surprises anyone."

They stared at the fire for several minutes before Andy broke the silence. She put her arm around her youngest sister and said, "At least Matthew is still going to marry you. That's good."

Jack couldn't hold back her tears any longer. She fell into Andy's arms, sobbing quietly. Jay and Sam came to stand beside her, rubbing her back and arms.

"It still only gets worse," Jack gasped out between sobs. "The worst part of the whole situation is what happened between Matthew and me."

"What?" Andy turned and looked at Jack. Suddenly she knew that major pieces of this puzzle were still missing. "What exactly are you talking about?"

Sam handed Jack a tissue, and she wiped her eyes and nose before answering. "I feel like I'm more myself with Matthew than anyone that I've ever met before. It's like our hearts just connect."

"Oh, no." Jay's voice held alarm.

"Quiet," Andy commanded her.

"When I'm near him," Jack went on in a far-away voice, "I feel as though I can hardly breathe. I see nothing but him. In a room filled with people, I see no one but him."

"Oh, this is really, really bad," Jay announced in a worried tone.

"Be quiet, Jay!" Andy scolded her angrily.

"I feel like I'm watching a movie out of focus." Jack's voice was desperate and empty. "I've never felt more helpless or confused in my life."

Sam put her arms around her younger sister, and embraced her lovingly. "Jack, somehow it's all going to work out. I don't exactly know how…" she laughed softly, "but it will work out."

"Are you in love with him?" Andy asked her directly.

"It sure sounds like she's in love with him," Jay stated confidently.

"Quiet!" Andy glared impatiently at Jay. "I'm getting ready to dump you in the lake."

"He's like this wonderful memory that I'll never forget. It's like something that I can't erase. It's written on my heart forever. All my times with him keep replaying in my mind. I can't escape them."

The pain in Jack's voice cut deep. All the sisters hurt for her.

"Oh, boy…" Jay muttered under her breath.

Andy just stared at her, and Jay stayed quiet. "Jack, do you love him?" Andy persisted.

"Yes," Jack admitted quietly.

"I told you she's in trouble," Jay frowned at Andy knowingly.

"It doesn't matter, Jay," Jack continued in a sad tone. "Matthew will never be mine. He's like a touch of heaven that I can't ever keep. And do you know what?" Jack said as she looked at Jay angri-ly. "That's probably the cruelest kind of love. When you actually experience true love, so that you know, without a shadow of a doubt, deep down in your heart, exactly what you're missing. You know exactly what's been taken from you. My heart will never be the same."

All the sisters were quiet. They all sat in front of the little fire, not able to think of a thing to say. Finally, Andy asked curiously, "Exactly what did happen between you and Matthew?"

Jack sighed loudly. "He was talking about love, a deep, committed love that's rooted in the Lord. Our eyes locked," Jack rattled on quickly, "and we couldn't take our eyes off each other. We just keep staring at each other. And then, he leaned forward, and was going to kiss me."

"Really?" Sam asked in shock.

"You are so far out in left field, Sam, it isn't even funny," Jay shook her head in an annoyed way. "Jack and Matthew have been attracted to each other since they met. Why is it so surprising that he wants to kiss her?"

Andy narrowed her eyes at Jay for a moment, and then turned to Jack. "What stopped him from kissing you?"

"Flyer and Docker," Jack laughed quietly, and she patted the dogs who had fallen asleep beside her. "As our lips were about to meet, the dogs flattened Matthew for his fudge bag."

The girls couldn't contain their laughter. "Talk about timing," Andy giggled as she stroked Docker's soft head.

"Would you call it good timing, or bad timing?" Sam asked quietly.

Jack blew out a long, deep breath. "I really wanted him to kiss me."

"I knew it," Jay stated triumphantly. "They love each other."

"So, what are you going to do?" Sam asked seriously.

"What do you mean by do?" Jack asked in a puzzled tone.

"She means," Jay said forcefully, "are you going to dump that jerk Bradley and marry Matthew."

Silence filled the air, and Jay groaned loudly. "I don't know who I'm more disappointed in. Bradley for being such a jerk, or you for not dumping him."

"It's not that easy, Jay," Jack shot back angrily.

"Actually," Jay became impatient and heated, "I think the decision is remarkably easy. It seems black and white to me."

Again a heavy silence filled the air. Sam's quiet, non-threatening voice broke through. "Jack, did you ever think that you're being unfair and dishonest to Bradley?"

"How do you see that?" Jack asked, trying hard to control the anger that was building up in her.

"You're lying to him." The conviction in Sam's voice was strong. "You don't love him." She paused and poked at the fire with a stick. "I don't think you've ever loved him more than a brother. It's a lie for you to marry him and tell God and the world you love him…when you really don't."

"That's an excellent point, Sam!" Jay grew excited. "And, I just bet you could add sin to this list."

"I'm not even sure I want to know how you see that." The frustration oozed out of every word Jack spoke.

"I'll tell you anyway." Jay waved a hand at her sister. "OK. Here it goes. You're going to love this. I believe this is one of those rare moments when

I'm thinking above my ability." The sisters couldn't help but laugh at Jay.

"I believe that if you marry Bradley it's a sin for a couple of reasons. First, you don't even love him, Jack. You know it's got to be pretty obvious when even I can see that. Everyone knows you shouldn't marry someone that you don't love. The second reason that it's a sin is Bradley is so clearly not God's choice for you. A blind man could see that. It appears that you're more interested in pleasing Grandpa Miller than you are in pleasing God. And that," Jay added, shaking her head, "is a definite sin. You shouldn't want to please anyone more than you want to please God." Jay paused, and then said quietly, "I think there's a Bible verse that says something like that."

All three sisters stared at Jay for a full minute before commenting. Jay had a big smile plastered to her face. "I know," she exclaimed proudly, "this revelation is really remarkable for me."

"I hate to say it," Andy sounded completely amazed, "but she's right."

Jack couldn't say anything. Her sister's words convicted her deeply. Finally she mumbled, "I never thought of it that way."

Jay laughed, "I'll just bet you didn't." She still sounded quite pleased with herself.

"OK, listen, Plato," Andy looked hard at Jay, "your thoughts were good—amazingly right on. But putting all that aside…"

Jay interrupted her, "Do we have to put it aside so quickly? A moment like this doesn't happen very often for me. Actually," Jay paused and ran a hand through her short brown hair, "a moment like this has never happened for me."

The girls had to laugh. Jay was honestly funny.

"What I was trying to say," Andy watched Jay closely to make sure she wouldn't interrupt, "was that now that Jack has been confronted with the truth of the situation and knows the truth in her heart, we need to pray for her. We should pray that God gives her the courage to make the right decisions."

"What decisions are there to make?" Jay asked in a puzzled tone. "Jack loves Matthew, and we think that he probably loves her. She should dump that bonehead Bradley and marry Matthew."

"It's not that easy." Jack was openly struggling. "You're right. I do love Matthew. I think I have for a long time, from a distance."

"Well, Sister…" Jay patted her on the back, "it's time you closed the distance."

Ten

$\mathscr{A}$s Matthew made his way up the driveway to the Inn, his stomach was in knots. He had purposely avoided coming within a mile of Sugar Creek Inn for the last two weeks. He didn't want to risk having to face Jack, but now Roy and Ray Hobson had asked him to come by, and being their pastor he couldn't very well say no.

He carefully avoided the grand front entrance of the sprawling Victorian mansion, and took the little brick path that led toward the back. As he was passing the screen door that led to the kitchen, he heard someone call his name. He stopped and looked toward the door. A moment later it swung open.

"Hi, Matthew," Melina Miller said cheerfully. "We haven't had the pleasure of your company in quite some time."

Matthew smiled kindly at Mrs. Miller. She and her daughter Andy looked so similar they could pass as sisters. "Yes," Matthew replied taking a few steps toward the door, "things have been very busy with Vacation Bible School starting up next month."

"Well," Melina's voice was welcoming, "you really should come in the kitchen for a moment. Andy and I just finished baking a batch of double chocolate cookies. Come in and try some."

"That sounds like a good offer, Mrs. Miller." As Matthew climbed the brick steps up to the kitchen, the smell of freshly baked chocolate cookies attacked his senses and drew him into the house.

Melina offered Matthew a plate of warm cookies. He took two and thanked her. As he dropped into a ladder-back chair in the large country kitchen, he turned slightly and noticed Jay sitting on the counter. She had a chunk of chocolate in one hand and a jar of peanut butter in the other.

Matthew smiled and then laughed at the sight of her. "You look like a little kid trying to make Reese's."

Jay looked up from the jar of peanut butter she was holding and laughed. "Want to try some?" She waved a chunk of chocolate that was thickly covered with peanut butter in his direction.

"Sorry," he said, waving off her offer, "that mess you're holding there is no competition for these cookies."

"Well, Pastor," Andy looked disgustedly at her sister, "you don't know what you've really turned down. Jay is the worst chocoholic I know. There is no more milk chocolate in the house, so she's reduced herself to eating baker's chocolate."

Matthew's mouth dropped open slightly, and the ladies laughed at the shocked expression that had spread across his face. "Baker's chocolate?" he scrunched up his face. "Isn't that really bitter?"

The women all laughed again before Jay spoke for herself. "You see," she began logically, "there is a method to my madness. I take a chunk of the baker's chocolate and dunk it into the peanut butter. Then, for the finale, I dunk it into sugar!"

"That sounds like one great big stomachache to me." Matthew wrinkled his face at Jay.

The Miller women were howling and Matthew had to join in. As he looked at the combination of glop that Jay was holding, he couldn't help but laugh.

When the laughter died down, Jay spoke adamantly. "It's really not that bad!"

"Yeah, but it doesn't sound that good, either!" Matthew smiled as he munched on his second cookie.

"It's not the best," Jay admitted honestly. "But then again," she had to laugh at herself, "it's not the worst thing I've ever eaten either! In my desperate condition, this is actually not so bad."

"You're awful!" Andy proclaimed disgustedly. "When Jay gets on a chocoholic run, she'll drink the chocolate milk syrup without any milk!"

"Yuck!" Matthew cast a wary look at her. "That's grosser than what you're doing now."

Everyone laughed. "There are more stories…," Andy volunteered quickly.

"I'm not sure I want to hear any more. I don't think my stomach could take them." Matthew stood. He took his wallet out of his back pocket. He pulled out five dollars and handed it to Jay. "Do the world a favor, Jay, and go buy yourself some chocolate bars."

Andy and Melina laughed hard. Jay smiled and eagerly accepted the money. "Thanks, Matthew. Can I borrow your car to run down to the store?"

Matthew pulled his keys out of his pocket and tossed them toward her. "Have fun!" he said as she ran out the door.

"Sometimes, I don't know where that child comes from," Melina joked. "She's so different from the others."

Everyone laughed again. As Matthew grabbed another cookie, he inquired about the Hobson brothers.

"Oh, they're probably on the back porch arguing over a game of checkers." Andy had started cleaning up the kitchen. "They can be fiercely competitive."

As Matthew went outdoors to make his way to the back porch, he wondered where Jack was. He was relieved he hadn't run into her, but just the same, he couldn't help but think about her.

As Matthew rounded the corner of the large white house, he saw the Hobson brothers sitting on their usual end of the porch. As if Andy had been spying on them, she was right about their argument. They were in a heated debate over the checkerboard.

When he climbed the wide, white porch steps, the arguing stopped. The old brothers greeted him politely, as if nothing had been going on.

"Nice afternoon, Pastor," Roy commented cheerfully. Ray looked a little less cheerful. Matthew couldn't hide his smile. Ray had probably lost the argument.

"Thanks for inviting me over, Boys. This sure is a beautiful spot." Matthew turned and scanned the lake. The Inn was located in the central section of the lake and tucked nicely into a safe harbor. Matthew felt it was one of God's special spots.

"There sure are a variety of houses around Eagle Lake," Matthew said thoughtfully as he gazed across the water.

"Ah-yup," Ray said in his thickest Maine accent. "We sure got ourselves variety."

"Yup," Roy agreed quickly, nodding his head slightly. "We've got ourselves inns, cottages, and camps."

Matthew glanced back at the brothers with a confused expression. "What's the difference between cottages and camps?"

The old brothers' eyes lit up at the question, and a low chuckle escaped them. "Well, let's see..." Ray pretended to be thoughtful. "Your basic cottage would be run by someone like Martha Stewart."

"Yup," Roy agreed, "and your camp would be run by someone like Betty Crocker."

Matthew smiled broadly. He could tell he was in for one of Roy and Ray's famous running dialogues. They were a comical pair.

"Your cottage is going to have folks like the Kennedys," Ray continued.

"While your camp people are more I Love Lucy type fans."

"Cottage people belong to country clubs and own yachts..."

"Camp people belong to hunting clubs and own canoes and inflatable boats..."

"Cottages have clam bakes and drink white wine..."

"Camps have hot dog roasts and drink bug juice…"

"Cottage people attend classical concerts in the park…"

"Camp people sing songs around the late night bonfires…"

"Cottages are located around beautiful, scenic views…"

"Camps can be located near a porta potty or out-house."

Matthew was laughing so hard that his sides ached. "You two should have been on the road doing comedy!"

"You think we're funny, Son?" Ray asked seriously, pretending not to know. His eyes sparkled, revealing the laughter he felt inside.

"I think no one knows how to tell a story like you two." Matthew smiled at the two brothers.

"I always liked that boy," Roy added quickly.

"Yup. I even think we'll let him become an official Mainer."

Just then Jack came through the back door carrying a tray with iced tea and cookies. At the sight of Matthew, she halted in her tracks. Matthew seemed unable to move as well. Just the sight of this woman he loved seemed to throw his emotions into a tailspin.

"I thought the fireworks weren't going to start until the Fourth of July," Roy mumbled jokingly.

"Looks like they started early this year." Ray smiled at Jack.

"I didn't expect to see you here," Jack said softly to Matthew.

Before he could answer, Roy and Ray Hobson said in unison, "I just bet you didn't!" The brothers started to laugh, while Jack only turned bright red.

"I'm sorry, Jack," Roy apologized quickly. "We didn't mean to embarrass you. You see, Ray and I are so desperate for company here that we invited Matthew to the Inn for a visit."

Jack nodded and then looked back at Matthew. She didn't want to take her eyes off him. She had missed his company so much. Her eyes began to tear up, as the ache in her heart grew. A love that can never be yours is too painful to bear, Jack thought as she turned her head away from him.

"I'm starting to feel like a third wheel here, Ray," Roy whispered loudly.

"Maybe we should leave them alone." Ray sounded awkward and uncomfortable.

Matthew smiled at the brothers and then turned to Jack. "That's not a bad idea, Fellers. Jack, would you like to go for a walk down to the boathouse for a couple of minutes?"

Jack nodded. She set the tray of refreshments in front of the Hobsons, and silently headed toward the lake with Matthew.

"I've missed seeing you, Matthew," Jack blurted out suddenly.

Matthew smiled tenderly. "I've missed seeing you too."

They walked around the side of the boathouse, shielding themselves from the Inn's view. Sitting down on some large rocks, they sat quietly for a few minutes.

Jack was the first to break the silence. "How have you been?"

"Hanging in there." He glanced at her seriously. "Are you and Bradley still engaged?"

Jack slowly nodded. "Yes," she answered in a reluctant tone.

Matthew's voice took an emotional dive. "Then I think I'm doing awful." As he turned to look at Jack, he saw her eyes were filled with tears.

"Jack," Matthew said earnestly, "forgive me. I shouldn't have said that. I didn't mean to get you upset."

Jack sighed loudly. "It's OK, Matthew. I'm really confused about the whole issue."

"Do you want to talk about it?" Matthew asked compassionately

"You sure you want to listen to it?" Jack hesitated. As she looked at Matthew, he nodded, and she slowly began. "According to my sisters, my reasons for marrying Bradley are all wrong."

"Are they?"

"They say that I don't love Bradley. They say I'm being dishonest to him by marrying him." Matthew looked at Jack thoughtfully. "Before you comment here, let me tell you the rest." Matthew nodded, and Jack slowly continued.

"They say that I'm not marrying God's choice for my life. They say that I'm committing a sin by not marrying God's choice."

Matthew had never taken his eyes off Jack as she spoke. He slowly cleared his throat, and then said quietly, "I'm not sure what you want me to say, Jack."

"How do you feel? Do you think they're right?"

It was clear that the young woman next to him was struggling. He knew he should reach out and try to help her. Yet at the same time, he was so torn up inside, he wasn't sure that was possible.

"Jack," Matthew said quietly, "I think whether or not you love Bradley is a question only you can answer. I believe that if you're honest with yourself, and ask for God's wisdom, you'll find the answers to your questions."

Jack nodded and then stared out across the lake. She could see Mailboat Eddie heading this way with Sam, and she smiled. Eddie tooted his horn and waved at them when he saw them. Both Matthew and Jack waved back.

"Have they been seeing a lot of each other?"

"Yes," Jack admitted cheerfully. "Eddie has been coming by the Inn almost every day. Sam is walking around on Cloud Nine!"

Matthew smiled at the thought. Yet a second later, his face turned serious. "Jack, can I ask you something personal?"

"Yes," she answered as she studied Matthew.

"How come you're not on Cloud Nine? Most brides-to-be that I meet are flying. How come you're not?"

"That's a complicated question to answer." Jack instantly looked away from Matthew's probing eyes.

"Do you want to try to answer it?"

"No, Matthew. I don't," Jack's tone was firm.

"Why not?" Matthew asked, surprised.

"Maybe it's because if I admitted the truth to myself, I'd have a whole lot of trouble dealing with it," Jack answered honestly.

Matthew was quiet for a minute and then said sincerely, "Jack, I pray for you every day. You're never far from my mind." He wanted to add that she was never far from his mind or his heart, but Matthew knew that he must try to contain his feelings.

"Thank you," Jack replied in a choked-up voice.

As she got up to go, Matthew called to her. "Jack, as far as the other thing that your sisters said, about you marrying the wrong guy…"

Jack looked at him hesitantly, and managed a slight nod.

"I believe God is very disappointed when people marry the wrong choice. Since He created us, don't you think He knows who's best for us?"

Jack slowly nodded. "Yes, I do."

"Did that help?" Matthew asked in a caring voice.

"Not really," Jack laughed nervously.

"That's probably because no one can make your decisions for you, Jack."

Jack nodded thoughtfully.

"And, Jack," Matthew added quickly as she turned to walk away, "that includes Grandpa Miller. He shouldn't be making decisions for you, either."

Jack turned back and stared at Matthew as though the idea had never occurred to her. She managed to sluggishly nod her head, before turning to walk away.

As Matthew watched her disappear around the boathouse, he felt his heart go with her. He wished he could put her on a sailboat and sail her away from her haunting past. Yet he knew, down inside, that unless she faced the dark problems in her past, she would never truly be free from them.

As he walked toward the back porch to face Roy and Ray, his steps were measured and heavy. "Boys," Matthew's voice was burdened, "do you mind if I come back again some other time?"

"No, Matthew," Roy was understanding.

"Thanks. I'm not feeling so well today."

As the old brothers watched the young pastor drive away, Roy turned to Ray and asked doubtfully, "Sickness?"

"Yup," Ray said, nodding sadly. "He's got the worst kind. Poor Matthew's got sickness of the heart."

Eleven

$\mathscr{B}$y the beginning of July, the Inn was packed to capacity. All ten guest rooms were full. There were families with children, young couples, older couples, and of course the Hobson brothers. However Jack's favorite guests of all time, that she looked forward to seeing every day, were the black bears that would visit and play on their hammocks and swing sets.

After watching these acrobatic animals, Jack understood how circus bears came to be. They were natural clowns, with the hearts of energetic four-year-olds.

They loved to climb up on the hammocks and swing back and forth, and it was not a gentle, lulling type of motion. The movement they created was similar to the action you'd see at an amusement park. The bears clearly enjoyed the thrill of the ride. Jack often joked with her sisters about feeling motion sickness just watching them.

Over the years, many of the same bears returned to the Inn's playground. Roy and Ray

started naming the bears after famous baseball leg-
ends, and the names stuck. Everyone had a
favorite. Dad and Roy liked Mickey Mantle. He
had a strong, brawny build, and walked around
like he owned the joint. Ray and Andy liked Babe
Ruth. He was definitely the biggest clown out of
the bunch. Mom and Ethan like Joe DiMaggio
because he carried himself with class. Two new
bear cubs named Willie Mays and Hank Aaron
won the hearts of Jack and Sam. The two young
bear cubs were always chasing after each other and
wrestling. The bears of baseball were the most
entertaining activity to watch on the lake. They
had a style, class, and agenda all of their own. They
never failed to bring a smile to their audience.

Other guests, equally famous, but not as well
liked, were the Brady boys. Ken and Cody Brady,
now eight and nine, had been coming to the Inn for
the first week in July since they were babies. They
were the most argumentative, fiercely competitive,
annoying, loud, pushy, unpleasant children that
Sugar Creek Inn had ever hosted. Their parents
seemed helpless to control them. During their
week-long visit, which always seemed much
longer, the two boys crossed every line, boundary,
and off-limits area that they weren't supposed to. If
there was a No Trespassing sign, they'd trespass. If
there was a Do Not Enter sign, they'd enter. If the

sign said Keep Out, they'd make it a point to go in. It was a week the Millers always dreaded.

"This year," Max declared in a determined voice at the weekly Saturday morning meeting, "we are going to be on top of those Brady boys. I've come to resent their week here more than any other week. This year," Max said forcefully, "I give you each permission to defend the fort."

A loud cheer went up from the girls. "Oh, I never thought I'd live to hear those words!" Jay's excitement rocketed. "I need some rope, some crazy glue and," she added as an afterthought, "a shot gun would probably be good, too."

Everyone broke out laughing. "I am not giving you a license to torture them, Jay," Max's tone was amused. "I've got an excellent plan of action this year. We will beat them at their own game."

"That's why I need rope, crazy glue, and a gun, Dad," Jay demanded seriously. "You can't expect a soldier to fight a war without an arsenal."

"That's not what I had in mind," Max replied sternly. "I'm not looking for a lawsuit from the Bradys."

"You're no fun at all!" Jay whimpered.

"Your Mother probably agrees," Max smiled at his second daughter, "but my plan is more diplomatic. I'm planning on making you girls generals over Ken and Cody."

"Dad, why are you only staring at Jay and me?" Jack asked suspiciously.

"Because you two are going to be the generals. You'll each be in charge of one boy."

"What about Andy and Sam?" Jay inquired quickly. She did not like how this plan was playing out.

"Sam is too gentle. Ken and Cody would eat her alive. We need Andy around here to cook. Besides, she has Nicholas to watch."

"I don't like this!" Jay announced in an adamant tone. "It's totally unfair. You're not giving us permission to kill them, or at the very least, inflict bodily harm. I'm not suggesting anything permanent…" Her voice trailed off thoughtfully.

Everyone laughed. With the Brady boys, your mind did run along those lines. Even though you'd never act on it, it was always fun to talk about what you'd like to do to them.

"Basically," Jack said, eyeing her father closely, "you're asking Jay and me to baby-sit them for the week. Not fair. I strongly object."

"Overruled," Max stated calmly. "I think you and Jay could be activity directors for those boys, and keep them out of trouble."

"You're asking the impossible!" Jay was thoroughly disgusted.

"Maybe so," Max agreed thoughtfully, "but I've given this a lot of thought, and I feel it's worth a try." He paused and scanned the group for a second. "If any of you have a better idea, I'm open to it."

"I have great ideas!" Jay protested. "You just don't like any of them."

"That's probably because what you have in mind is against the law!" Max smiled at Jay.

"Look on the bright side." The girls immediately noted the forced cheerfulness in Melina's voice. "You and Jack are being relieved of all your duties at the Inn this week."

"Why am I not feeling relieved?" Jack mumbled.

"Because," Jay spat out angrily, "we're being thrown from the pot into the fire."

"If I were you, I'd run a boot camp for those boys." Max eyed them seriously. "Set up a regular schedule. Load your days full of activities. I believe that will help a great deal."

"I believe a gun will help a great deal," Jay said heatedly.

Max looked at Jay sternly. "No weapons. You're not allowed, under any circumstances, to harm them."

"I wasn't planning on doing anything that would permanently harm them." Jay couldn't hide her irritation. "Oooh," she suddenly asked excitedly, "how about a stun gun. It wouldn't harm them permanently. It would be great!"

"No." Max stared at Jay firmly. "I am trusting you two girls."

"That may not be wise." Sam chewed her bottom lip nervously. "Remember last year when the boys trashed Jay's room. She's still upset."

"Like you wouldn't be?" Jay asked Sam directly.

"Girls," Max was uncompromising, "the Bradys will be here in about two hours. I strongly suggest you put your heads together and make some plans."

As Jay and Jack sat on the back porch steps complaining about their assignment, Roy and Ray were howling. "This is going to be the most entertaining year yet! Yes, sir—the best!"

"Well," an annoyed tone hissed through Jay's clenched teeth, "if Dad says we're generals, then I intend to dress like one. I have some army fatigues up in my room. You want some?"

Jack laughed. "No. I'll stay in my tee shirt and shorts."

When Ken and Cody arrived, the girls were ready for them. Max explained their plan to Mr. And Mrs. Brady, and they readily agreed. Boot Camp was about to begin.

For the first day, the girls decided to pack a lunch and take Ken and Cody hiking up Greyson

Mountain. Jack found small backpacks for each of the boys, so each person carried his own gear.

At the base of the mountain, the first challenge hit. Cody and Ken started in with their routine of: I can do this better than you. I can do this faster than you. I am stronger than you. And so on.

"That's it!" Jay firmly turned both boys around to face her. "That is enough! If I hear one more argument from either one of you, I'm taking away your lunches."

"You can't do that!" Ken protested in a snotty way. "Our parents have paid for them. This food is ours!"

Jay smirked at them. "Well, here's a little news-flash for you, Pal. Your parents aren't here, are they?"

Both boys looked momentarily concerned. Jay enjoyed the look of fear in their eyes. For a second, victory was hers.

"I think," Jack added seriously, "that since your parents paid for the lunches, we should give them back to your parents."

"Yeah, but they wanted us to have them!" Cody whined loudly.

"Then I suggest you follow the rules here." Jay leaned toward them. With her army fatigues on, she did look intimidating. "You're bound to be very hungry if you don't. Get the message?"

Both boys nodded in unison. They looked as though they believed Jay's threat just enough to obey her.

"Then let's hike," Jay announced and began climbing up the path.

For the next hour the boys were remarkably good. Jack felt the main reason was because they were afraid of Jay. She smiled to herself. A little healthy fear never hurt anyone!

The model behavior didn't last long enough. When they paused to pick blueberries in a large meadow, Ken and Cody started chucking rocks at the bears.

"STOP THAT!" Jay and Jack shouted at the same time.

"Why should we?" Cody demanded arrogantly.

"Because," Jay marched up to the boys, "it's mean!"

"Besides that," Jack said seriously, "if you get them mad, they'll chase us. Remember, Jay and I can run faster than you and Ken."

"So," Cody answered in his usual bratty tone, "what's that supposed to mean?"

Jack looked him squarely in the eye. "It means that since we run faster than you...the bears will get to you first."

The light of understanding began to dawn on young Cody's face. He paled visibly.

"Black bears don't eat kids," Ken stated as if he were an expert on the subject.

"You want to bet? Obviously you don't know a lot about bears." Jay shook her head at them. "Angry bears do violent things. Trust me. Don't throw rocks at them or you'll be on your own once they start heading our way."

The boys looked sulkily at each other. The girls had implanted enough fear in them to make them behave, and that was the main idea.

After another hour of steady hiking through the forest, they reached the mountaintop lake. It was actually nothing more than a large pond with a dozen Canadian geese on it, but the grassy hill just above the lake was a pleasant place to stretch out and have lunch.

As they ate their lunches, they watched the flock of geese. A few minutes later, Cody stood up, picked up a rock, and began his wind up toward the geese. Jay quickly grabbed his wrist before the rock left his hand.

"I can see you have absolutely no respect for wildlife," Jay seethed angrily.

Cody laughed obnoxiously. "Don't try to tell me that the geese are going to come after me and chase me!"

Jay stared him down for a minute. "I hadn't thought of that. They do chase people, and they can be very mean." She paused again, and then spoke crossly, "I don't know what it is with you and rocks. I don't know why you like to throw them at animals. It's a rotten thing to do."

"I don't like geese," Cody acted as if this reason would justify his actions.

"Well, you know something," Jay said hotly, "I don't particularly like you. You think you have the right to go around and hurt people and animals, or break anything you feel like smashing. It's wrong," Jay placed a strong hand on Cody's shoulder, "and it's going to stop now."

Cody rose defiantly to the command. "And if I don't?" His little blond eyebrows wiggled back at Jay skeptically.

Jay slowly cleared her throat. Jack could tell she was taking a minute to decide just how far to go. "I'm going to be honest with you, Cody. If Jack and I don't watch you and Ken, my Dad is going to send your family home. So," her eyes narrowed and her voice became hard, "if you annoy me too much, I'm going to refuse to watch you. Then you and your family will have to go home. It's your choice."

"No way!" both boys said at the same time in total disbelief.

"Yes, way," Jay's answer gave no room for doubt. "You know better than to think we're out here babysitting you because we actually want to."

"Listen," Jack added in a kinder tone, "what she said is true, but this week can be a lot of fun for all of us. Jay and I have all kinds of great activities planned. But," Jack spoke more firmly, "if you boys don't listen to us, you will have to go home. This is not a joke. Do you understand?"

The boys nodded seriously at Jack. "Good. Now if we hike this way for ten minutes," Jack pointed toward the right, "there is a great view of Eagle Lake."

The boys were genuinely impressed with the view. "Man, we can see boats and islands. This is so cool!" Ken quickly grew excited.

"How would you like to sail out to one of the islands?" Jack asked invitingly.

"Cody is still afraid of the water from last year," Ken looked at his younger brother.

"Why?" Jack rewound her memory trying to think of anything that happened last summer that would have caused this.

"Jay told him about the sharks in the lake," Ken replied in a factual voice.

Jay burst out laughing. "No. No. I remember this conversation clearly. I told him that there were sailboats on the lake called sharks."

The Brady boys glared at her accusingly. "That's not what you said!"

Jay shrugged. "That's what I thought I said. If you took it any other way, you simply misinterpreted what I said. It was an innocent mistake. Sorry for the confusion, Guys."

As Jay turned away from the boys, Jack saw her smile. Jack marched over to her sister and pulled her aside. "Jay," her tone was angry, "that was awful of you. You gave that little boy nightmares for a year!"

"Yeah, well sometimes those two just push me too far. I tend to exaggerate the facts when I get angry."

"You mean you've scared them with other stories?" Jack asked in concern, as she eyed the boys. They were looking at them curiously, but were wise enough to stay quiet.

Jay smirked. "There may have been an occasional story or two. I seriously doubt they were scared by anything I said."

"The shark story scared them for a year!" Jack threw her hands on her hips disgustedly.

"Consider it crowd control. I try to scare the little beasts enough to keep them under control."

"I can't believe you said that!" Jack tried hard to control the anger that was boiling inside her. "Listen, the boys know that if they're not good, they're going home. Why don't we take this week and try to be a positive influence in their lives. I imagine they get enough negative influence at home."

"Now that's something that I believe. They're little juvenile delinquents!"

"Jay," Jack tried earnestly to reason with her older sister, "I agree with you. They can be pretty awful. Still, we may be the only light of Jesus they see. We should be praying for them."

"I am praying for them," Jay said heatedly. "I'm praying that I won't kill one of the little buggers before the week is over!"

"Jay!" Jack's voice held a clear warning tone, and Jay knew she had crossed the line.

Jay stared at her sister for a moment, and then nodded her head. "OK. If the little brats stay fairly nice, I will promise not to kill them."

"I was looking for a little more than that. Try to be positive with them."

"Listen," Jay impatiently ran a hand through her short hair, "I think promising not to kill them is a pretty positive thing on my part."

"Please," Jack begged. "I really feel strongly about this. We don't let them get away with anything, but at the same time, we try to reach out to them."

Jay stared at Jack for a full minute before saying a thing. "I think I can go along with that, but don't push me too far."

"Thanks." Jack lovingly threw an arm around her sister.

"I think it's a little premature to thank me yet. We've only had the boys for the day," Jay eyed them skeptically.

The rest of the day was relatively uneventful. The next day was Sunday. The Miller clan, along with the Brady family, went to church. Matthew finally got to meet the famous Brady brothers.

"Would you like some help with the boys throughout the week?" Matthew asked Jack. "I've worked with a lot of boys' camps over the years."

"Hey, I'll never turn down any help concerning Cody and Ken." Jack smiled at Matthew. "Why don't you plan on sticking around after lunch today. I'm sure you can help us think of some way to entertain them."

As fate would have it, after lunch the sky broke open and torrents of rain fell. "I guess we're going to have to think of something to do with the boys inside." Jack couldn't hide her regret. "Dad's not going to like this."

"Why don't we go swimming?" Matthew volunteered.

"It's raining," Jack scrunched her nose up at him.

"So?" Matthew replied, scrunching up his nose right back at her.

"We'll get wet," Jack complained.

Matthew laughed hard. "Jack, I hate to be the one to break the news to you after all these years, but when you go swimming you do tend to get wet."

Jack laughed, and smiled at her friend. She had missed Matthew and his quick sense of humor. "It's going to be cold."

"So we won't go for long."

"OK," Jack nodded in agreement, "but when I start turning into a Popsicle, I'm outta there."

"Deal," Matthew shook her hand.

The boys were thrilled. A game of water tag quickly got under way. Base was the long metal slide, and Jack was sticking to it like glue.

"You're shivering." Matthew eyed her with concern.

"The water's cold," Jack complained, sounding as happy as a wet cat might have.

Matthew laughed. "If you'd move around, you would be warmer."

"If I move around, you'll tag me."

"I'm certainly going to try," Matthew admitted.

Jack climbed the long metal ladder that led to the top of the slide. Matthew was waiting for her at the bottom. Just as she started down the slide, Cody slipped on a rock and screamed out. As Matthew started to swim toward the boy to help him, he made the mistake of passing right in front of the end of the slide. Jack's foot collided with Matthew's face. Just before Jack plunged into the water, she heard Matthew cry out in pain.

After she surfaced, Jack immediately noticed two things. Jay had both boys and was heading toward the Inn, and Matthew was clinging to one of the extension poles on the slide. Jack swam over to him quickly.

"Matthew, I'm so sorry." Jack's voice was instantly apologetic and full of concern. "Did I break anything?"

"I'm not sure if you broke anything or not." The pain in Matthew's voice said enough. "I feel like I have broken my nose and had my left eyeball pushed all the way back through my head."

As Jack helped Matthew back to the Inn, she kept apologizing profusely. "I'm sorry, Matthew. I'm so sorry. This is all my fault."

"Jack," Matthew said kindly, "your apologizing is worse than the pain. Please stop."

"OK," Jack answered nervously. "I'll stop apologizing. I'm sorry."

Matthew stopped and looked at her humorously. "You even apologize for apologizing too much. That's really bad."

Jack looked as though she were trying not to cry. "Jack," Matthew said tenderly, "it's really OK."

Max Miller showed up on the porch and helped Matthew in. "What happened?" His voice was full of alarm.

"Jack creamed the pastor!" Cody volunteered quickly in an excited voice.

"Yeah, you should have seen it. She just plowed right over him," Ken added.

"Go get changed," Jay commanded the brothers, and they took off.

"It was an accident, Max." Matthew held his nose gently. "I'm going to get changed, and then I think I'll lie down with some ice on my face."

Jack and Jay got changed as well. By the time they got downstairs, Roy, who used to be a general country doctor, was examining Matthew. Matthew was lying on a couch in the den with Roy bent over him.

"You didn't break the nose, Son." Roy's manner was gentle and kind. "But it sure did take quite a beating. So did that left eye. Here's some Tylenol. You're going to need it."

People came in to stare at Matthew and hear the details of the accident throughout the afternoon. Jay had kindly volunteered to watch the Brady boys so Jack could stay with Matthew.

"Gee," Matthew's voice was weary, "I certainly know how to get a lot of attention. By the way, I think you were really trying to blind me so I could-n't give you driving lessons. Nice try!"

"Driving lessons?" Jack asked in a clueless tone.

Matthew laughed. "Yeah, you know, you behind the wheel, me instructing... I just want you to know I haven't forgotten about them."

"Well I have!" Jack responded quickly.

"Jack, we're going to have to talk about this sooner or later."

"Make it later."

"Jack, you're making this so hard on yourself. Once the swelling goes down, I feel we should hit the road."

Jack looked like she was going to cry. She was biting her lower lip, and her eyes were filled with tears. "I can't believe I did that to you."

Matthew slowly took her hand, and held it gently within his own. "I'm going to be OK, Jack. The swelling and the bruises will make me look tough." Matthew smiled at her. "Roy says the cut above my left eye may turn into a really cool scar."

Jack had to laugh at Matthew's enthusiasm. "Pastor Bishop, you have a strange way of looking at injuries."

"I'm a guy," Matthew shrugged, as if no further explanation were needed. He squeezed her hand and then slowly let it go.

Jack missed his touch instantly. "You look tired," she noticed as she gazed into his brown eyes.

"Woman!" Matthew teased, "I've been through battle." Then Matthew laughed softly. "I think I lost the battle."

Jack had to laugh again. "Even when you're hurt, you're still funny." She paused, and fixed his disarrayed hair. "That says a lot about you, Matthew Bishop. You're one of a kind."

"I'm glad that you think so," Matthew studied her seriously. "I was sort of hoping you'd notice."

"I noticed right away." Jack took his hand in hers. She held it tightly, and closed her eyes for a minute. "Believe me, I noticed right away." She squeezed his hand and then released it slowly, in a regretful sort of way.

Their eye contact remained steady. Even though no words were spoken, through their eyes their hearts communicated the things that they couldn't allow themselves to say aloud.

"I want to say things to you. My heart is just aching to tell you things, but I can't. Because of your commitment to Bradley, it would be wrong of me." Matthew closed his eyes for a second as the frustration overwhelmed him.

Jack nodded understandingly. "I have things to say to you, too, Matthew." Jack took his hand again, and held it tightly. She could feel his love in his touch, and it warmed her heart. It was a feeling that she wanted to cling to forever. A second later her head caught up with her racing heart. Abruptly, as though someone had burned her, she dropped his hand, and looked at him with a confused expression.

"I feel so trapped." Her voice reminded him of a small helpless child. "I just don't know what to do."

"Jack," Matthew said urgently, "God does not give us the feeling of helplessness or entrapment. God promises us love, power, and a sound mind."

All Jack could do was nod.

"I'm praying for you. Turn to God, Jack. He will help you through your battle."

Jack felt the tears flowing down her cheeks. She simply nodded and then turned and left the room. Once again, she was not only leaving Matthew, but leaving her heart as well.

Except for the growing ache in Jack's heart, the rest of the week went well. She and Jay kept the Brady boys busy with activities ranging from hiking to lake sports. On the last night they had together, she and Jay got a chance to witness to the boys. They listened carefully but declined to make a commitment right away. Both of the boys agreed to think about Christ.

As the Millers watched the Bradys' car leave the Inn, Max proclaimed loudly what a success this year had been. "No one got stuck in the chimney, no one got stuck in the grandfather clock, and nothing that I know of was broken."

Jack smiled. The week had been surprisingly good. She had formed a genuine friendship with the boys and promised to write them. In her heart, she knew she would also pray for the boys daily. They had both come so close to accepting Christ. She didn't want the important decision to be forgotten because they had gone back home. Unless the boys accepted Christ, Jack knew that their hearts would never truly be home.

Twelve

"*You*," Bradley said, dropping his arm around Jack and then tightening his grip. "I've missed you!"

"You have?" Jack asked seriously.

"Yes, Jacilyn. I have." Bradley dropped his arm from around his girlfriend and looked at her directly. "I know it's been tough lately, with school and all. But," he wiggled his eyebrows at her as he pulled her into an embrace, "I'm officially graduated now. I'll be around so much that you'll be sick of me."

Jack tried to smile, but she couldn't. The whole image of being sick of Bradley seemed entirely too realistic. She felt as though her nightmare was about to be magnified by ten.

A minute later, Roy and Ray came through the screened porch and walked over to their self-designated rocking chairs. As Ray glanced around the porch, which he considered his personal domain, he seemed genuinely surprised to see Bradley there.

"You back?" he asked him sternly, with just a hint of disappointment in his tone.

"Yes, Sir," Bradley answered politely.

"Aw, shoot." Ray's voice was openly full of regret. "I thought you were gone for good."

Bradley eyed the brothers closely with annoyance spreading across his handsome face. "Now why would you say a thing like that?"

"Haven't seen much of you lately," Roy answered matter-of-factly.

"I've been at school," Bradley announced proudly, "and now I'm an official pastor!"

Both brothers stopped rocking and turned to stare at Bradley. "You're serious?" Roy was clearly shocked.

"Why, yes. Why wouldn't I be?" Bradley asked in a dejected tone.

"Just surprised you got through," Ray answered thoughtfully.

"And just what do you mean by that?" Bradley stood up and walked over to the Hobson brothers.

"Never figured you for pastor material." Roy was bold in his reply. "You don't seem to fit the bill."

"And what do you two old goats know? I graduated top of my class." Bradley grew angry. He told Jack that he would call her later and stormed off the porch, reminding her of how Nicholas acted when he was having a temper tantrum.

"I'm sorry, Guys," Jack apologized to the brothers, "he gets that way at times."

"Nothing for you to feel sorry about, My Dear," Roy smiled kindly.

"He shouldn't have spoken to you like that!" Jack balled her hands into fists angrily.

"You're right," Ray nodded thoughtfully "but I think it bothers me more that he called me an old goat. Other animals are more acceptable, but a goat? I don't like it!"

"Yes," Roy agreed with a twinkle in his eye. "He also called us old. I resent that, too!"

"We are old, Roy," Ray pointed out quickly.

"I believe," Roy's tone was indignant, "that is all a matter of perspective. From where I'm standing, I don't see myself as old. Now, Widow Vital on the other side of the lake," Roy stated with renewed energy, "she's old."

"She's 103!" Jack laughed at him.

"I know," Roy nodded. "She's old. I am not."

"If I were you," Jack smiled at them, "the next time Bradley starts getting disrespectful — I'd turn off my hearing aid."

"I didn't know you wore a hearing aid, Jack," Roy teased. "No one tells me anything around here any more!"

Jack laughed. The brothers were such characters that she couldn't help but laugh. "I don't wear a hearing aid, but you do. I'd shut it off the next time he gives you static."

"That's a good idea, Jack," Ray smiled thoughtfully. "I'll turn my hearing aid off, and simply tell the boy that I'm off the air! That should fix him!"

As Jack turned to go, Roy called out to her. "Oh, Jack," Roy's tone was enticingly vague, "if I were you, I'd ask that good old boy of yours just what his plans are for the future."

Jack turned to look at Roy with confusion clearly written across her face. "He's going to be the assistant pastor over at Sweetwater Creek. He's already got the position."

"I think plans have changed." Ray was quiet but adamant.

"OK, you two," Jack walked over to stand directly in front of them, "tell me what you know."

"Well, it's not like we were eavesdropping or anything, Jack." The embarrassment was beginning to show on Roy's face. "Bradley was using the hall phone, and I just happened to hear some of his conversation."

Jack narrowed her eyes at Roy accusingly. "Uh huh," she eyed them skeptically.

"Honest," Ray sounded like a little kid, "it wasn't our fault. The boy was practically yelling into the phone."

"You were hiding in the hall closet again, weren't you?" Jack asked suspiciously. "You know Dad told you not to do that anymore."

"I wasn't hiding," Roy declared smugly. "I was looking for my coat."

"Your coat isn't kept in the hall closet," Jack said quickly.

"Well, then, that's probably why I couldn't find the blasted thing," Roy shot back angrily.

"So, let me get this straight." Jack folded her arms across her chest. "You're in the hall closet, looking for a coat that isn't there, with the door shut." Jack had to laugh. They were worse than kids.

"Sometimes it happens that way," Roy said in a huff. "Listen, Miss High-and-Mighty, do you want to know what we found out or not?"

"OK. What did you hear?" Jack studied the brothers.

Roy instantly became excited, "Well, Bradley was talking to the Missions Board."

"The Missions Board?" Jack repeated, scrunching up her nose. "Are you sure?"

Roy rolled his eyes at her. "You know I'm good on my facts, Jack. How long have I been in the undercover business?"

Jack laughed. "As long as I've known you." Jack grew serious. "I wonder what Bradley is up too? He hasn't mentioned anything to me."

"I've no doubt of that!" Ray said hotly. "He wouldn't want you to know that…" Ray quickly clamped his mouth shut.

"Know what?" she asked targeting Ray with her eyes. "Exactly what is it that Bradley doesn't want me to know?"

The silence lingered for a moment before Roy cleared his throat loudly. "I don't believe it's our place to say."

"Oh, but it is your place to sit in the hall closet and listen to phone conversations? Come on! This is my future!" Jack was growing angry. "Don't play games with me."

"How does a future in missions sound to you?" Roy asked vaguely.

"What are you talking about here? Foreign or domestic?"

"Definitely foreign," Roy whispered, as he took a sudden interest in studying the porch flooring.

"You mean," Jack asked in an uncertain voice, "like leaving Maine to go to Vermont, or possibly New Hampshire?"

"Further." The resentment grew in Roy's voice.

A sick feeling began to wash over Jack. It was that feeling you get when you know that something bad is about to happen. This was going to be bad. She could feel it. "What?" Jack asked in a hesitant tone. "You mean like New Jersey or New York?"

"Further." Roy chewed his lower lip for a moment. "Now listen here, Jack. That's all I'm going to tell you. But, if I were you, I'd talk to

Bradley soon. He's planning your future, and in my eyes it doesn't look too bright."

"Just one more thing," Jack asked Roy in a hollow tone, "has anything permanent been arranged?"

"Yes, Jack," Roy said disgustedly, "I heard him say that he has signed contracts."

"He should have discussed this with me." Jack shook her head disbelievingly.

"We think so, Jack. That's why we knew we needed to tell you." Roy tightened his grip on the arms of his chair. "You definitely should have known about this."

Jack thanked them, and headed for her boat. She would sail over to Bradley's now and find out exactly what he had gotten them into. Jack angrily wondered in what way he had manipulated her life this time. And, she wondered as she climbed aboard her boat, exactly what she could do about it.

Thirteen

Jack wasn't able to find Bradley until the next day. It was the first day of Vacation Bible School and she and Bradley were scheduled to team-teach the sixth-grade boys.

As soon as Bradley entered the church, Jack zoomed in on him like a hawk going after its prey. "What are you up to?" she demanded, waving an insistent finger in his face. She was angry and decided that it was no use pretending that she wasn't. "You'd better tell me everything. I mean it."

"Good morning to you, too, Sweetheart," Bradley answered calmly, as he slowly backed away from the finger in his face. He casually drank his coffee as he thoughtfully studied his bride-to-be.

He was taking too long to answer. Jack decided he needed prompting. "I heard you were talking to the Foreign Missions Board. I want to know why?"

Shock spread across Bradley's face so quickly that he couldn't hide it. He delayed his answer a minute by taking an unnecessarily long gulp of coffee. "I was planning on discussing this with you later, Dear. I hardly think that this is the time or place."

"I think this is the time and place," Jack demanded heatedly. She had had the entire night to think about this, and by now she had worked herself into a thick, boiling stew.

"After V.B.S. today." Bradley's ultra calm tone only increased Jack's irritation. She hated when he treated her condescendingly, and right now he was acting more royal than the royal family themselves.

Bradley continued with measured, calculated words. "I have some great news to share with you. Why don't we go to lunch this afternoon, and we'll talk then?" It wasn't a question, or an invitation. It was a statement. Basically it was Bradley's way of saying: I'm not telling you anything right now. End of discussion.

The rest of the morning passed agonizingly slowly for Jack. She had trouble concentrating on the lessons and activities. The only thing that her mind wanted to focus on was what Bradley had done. Her mind tortured her as to what he had been up to.

Somewhere toward the end of the morning, it finally occurred to Jack that she should turn the situation over to God. "Oh, God," she prayed earnestly, as she prepared a tray full of snacks for her class, "I haven't been trusting in You. I've been completely panicking. Please help me to follow You, and stay calm."

The rest of the morning passed in a state of hurry and confusion, as only a day of Vacation Bible School can do. She dragged her boys to each activity and helped at each station with the process of set up, clean up, and repeat. After the closing song, Matthew sought her out.

"Are you OK there, Jack? You seem awfully distracted this morning. Are the boys being good for you?"

"The boys are great," Jack answered quickly.

"And the big guy?" Matthew questioned, referring to Bradley.

"Do you perform funerals, Matthew?" Jack asked him directly.

"It's a part of the job," Matthew looked at her curiously, taking a step closer to her.

"Well," Jack smiled for the first time that morning, "that's good, because I just might kill Bradley."

"OK…" Matthew tilted his head slightly, "premeditated murder. When are you going to decide?"

Jack laughed at him. "Probably this afternoon. I'll let you know if I need your services."

Matthew laughed. "OK. Maybe I'll catch you later, then."

"If I do decide to kill him," Jack narrowed her eyes, "I don't think I'll be in the best of moods."

"That's OK," Matthew nodded understandingly.

"Are you ready to go?" Bradley shouted at her from across the gym.

"Prince Charming awaits." Matthew found it difficult to plaster a smile on his face. Anything concerning Bradley was difficult for him these days.

"I think he's Prince Charmless," Jack mumbled, with anger growing in her voice.

Jack and Bradley made their way down to the wharf. They ordered sandwiches at Sally's, and took them to a bench that was at the water's edge.

"I'm famished!" Bradley held his sandwich as if he planned to devour it.

"What's the news?" Jack asked impatiently, leaving her own sandwich untouched.

"Eat first," Bradley commanded.

"I'd rather talk." She stared at him coldly.

"I'm starving!" Bradley complained.

"And because you are," Jack eyed him sternly, "I'll bet you'll be much quicker about telling me the news."

As Bradley was about to complain again, Jack reached over and picked up his sandwich. She simply held it over the water. "Talk now, or this is fish food."

"You wouldn't!" He stared at his sandwich with great concern.

"I'm feeling a bit like Jay right now. I actually think I might." She leaned closer to him, and said in a commanding tone, "Talk!"

Bradley stared longingly at his sandwich for a second. "Some interesting developments have arisen," he began slowly, never taking his eyes off his lunch.

"How interesting?" Jack asked flatly. "And, more importantly, how do they affect me?"

"Very interesting," he answered weakly "but I don't feel prepared to discuss it with you yet."

"Get prepared." Jack waved his sandwich over the water. "I want to hear it now, and I want to hear it straight."

"OK," Bradley agreed reluctantly. "I've had a wonderful missions opportunity. Actually, it's for both of us."

"Keep talking." She watched his every move suspiciously.

"You see, a professor of mine at the seminary felt that a short missions trip would look good on my resume. He feels it would help me land a larger church."

"You're kidding?" Jack spat out in shock.

"No," Bradley replied cautiously, "and, we'll get to travel."

"You know I hate to travel."

"This is a mission."

"I feel that my community is my mission. This is where I know God wants me. You know I feel that way, Bradley."

"It would only be for a year or two."

"Where?" Jack asked hesitantly.

Bradley suddenly appeared nervous. "I think we've discussed enough for one day. We should sleep on this and talk more another time."

"We'll talk more now," Jack insisted. "I know you signed us up to go somewhere. I want to know where."

Bradley shifted his feet tensely. "Africa. I signed us up for a five-year tour in Africa."

Jack's mouth opened, yet no words came out. Finally, after a minute, the full impact hit her. "You have got to be kidding!"

"Now calm down, Jacilyn. This is a good career move."

"I will not calm down. In case no one's ever told you before, you don't go into missions because it would look good on your resume, or be good for your career."

Jack flipped both sandwiches into the lake. "You go into missions and you go to Africa because you know that is where God is calling you to serve Him. As hard as you may find this to believe, it's not about you. It never has been. It's about serving God. You seem to be totally lost in understanding what an incredible privilege that is. And you know something? I know God wants me serving Him here at Sugar Creek. So, Pastor Bradley, I'm not going to Africa, because I know that's not where God wants me."

"You're just mad. You'll come around after you've had some time to think about it. You always do," Bradley added confidently.

As Jack turned to leave, Bradley stood up and grabbed her arm. "Jacilyn, sit down. You're making a scene."

"That's not a scene," Jack spat out angrily. "This is a scene!" She put her hands on his chest, and pushed him hard. He toppled backwards into the lake. When his blonde head surfaced, Jack looked him directly in the eye, and said, "That was a scene!"

Fourteen

As Jack prepared to make the four-mile walk back to the Inn, a familiar-sounding horn tooted behind her. Her father, in the Inn's old blue pickup truck, pulled up alongside her.

"Hop in, Stranger," he smiled warmly at Jack. "Let a handsome feller give you a lift."

"No thanks, Dad." Jack leaned against the door of the old Ford for a moment. "I think I need a good, long walk."

"I bet you do," Max laughed. Jack loved the way the corners of his eyes crinkled up when he laughed. "I saw Bradley walking out of the lake."

"Really?" Jack asked with the slightest measure of concern in her voice.

"Yes," Max laughed again. He turned in his seat to study her directly. " I thought it was kind of funny that he went swimming with his clothes on." He paused and cleared his throat. "You don't know anything about that, do you?"

"I pushed him in," Jack admitted without any remorse in her voice.

"I thought you might have." Max chuckled to himself again. "We should talk."

Jack scowled at her father. "I really don't feel like talking right now."

"Well, you see, that's a good thing," Max teased in his easy-going manner, "because I do. I'll talk and you'll listen, and we'll get along just fine. Especially," he added, laughing again, "if we stay away from the lake. I don't feel like going for a swim."

As Jack climbed into the old blue truck, she said seriously, "You know I'd never push you in the lake, Dad."

Max laughed loudly. "I bet Bradley thought the same thing. Boy, I bet he was surprised. I wish I had been there to witness it firsthand." Jack stared at her father with open astonishment. "Jack," his tone was disgusted, "Bradley had it coming to him. He was long overdue to be pushed in the lake by you. He earned it."

"You sound like my sisters. They aren't very fond of Bradley."

"Aren't very fond of him?" Max looked at her through narrowed eyes. "Why they downright despise the boy. You're the only one to see any good in him."

Max paused for a minute as they crossed Duck Path Bridge. It was a small covered bridge that spanned the Duck Path Brook. Oftentimes there would be children playing under the bridge, swimming and fishing, yet today all seemed quiet.

"Jack," Max's voice held concern in it, as he pulled the old truck to the side of the road, "I think it's high time I set the record straight. I know Grandpa Miller was crazy about Bradley. Yet, for the life of me, I can't understand why. Don't get me wrong," Max waved a hand at her, "he's a good-looking boy, and plenty smart enough, but he's severely lacking in the qualities that matter most to me. I don't think the boy has a caring, humble bone in his entire body."

Jack couldn't hide her surprise. Never had her father spoken so frankly with her about Bradley. "I just assumed you liked him."

"If I recall," Max spoke gently, "you never really asked. Besides, I assumed the same thing you did."

"What?" Jack asked him, not following what he had just said.

"I assumed you liked him, too." Max laughed kindly. "It never occurred to me that you didn't...until recently. I started watching you around Bradley, and then it just struck me that you don't love him, and probably don't even like him much." As Jack opened her mouth to argue, her father shook his head. "Jack, I know you too well.

You wear your feelings on your face, and they aren't that hard to read."

Jack didn't know what to say. He was right. The awkward silence grew, until her father spoke again.

"I wanted to give you space to make your own choices about your mate. Grandpa Miller was always too vocal with me on every girl I dated. I resolved not to do the same thing with you girls." Max sighed heavily. "Now I fear you're about to enter into a lifelong commitment with this lad. And," Max ran a troubled hand through his hair, "if I'm not missing my mark here, Jack, you're about to marry him because he's Grandpa's choice for you, not God's."

Jack stared at her father, completely dumbfounded. Max laughed quietly and shook his head slowly. "Didn't think your old Dad was so perceptive, did you?"

Jack was trying to hold back her tears. "I just thought...I mean," she was struggling with her unsteady voice, "that I guess I didn't realize it was so obvious."

Max took his daughter's hand, and squeezed it reassuringly. "Grandpa was a good man, Jack. We all loved him, and not a day goes by that I don't miss him." He exhaled loudly. "Jack, please don't marry Bradley because you feel obligated too."

Max sighed. "I never could figure out why you felt so obligated to Grandpa." Tears were rolling down Jack's face now. Instead of burying the issue, as she was so good at, she was being forced to face it. It was tearing her up inside.

"After the accident," Max's voice trailed on, "Grandpa seemed to have such a hold on you. Even from the grave..." Max shook his head in bewilderment. "If you're still feeling any guilt over the accident, you shouldn't," Max stated strongly.

"Jack," her father said urgently, turning Jack by the shoulders to face him, "he almost got you killed! Do you understand that? Nothing that happened was your fault. Not in the least. Good old Grandpa almost got you killed." Max sighed loudly. "Here you were struggling with guilt over the accident, while I was struggling not to hate my own father. He almost killed my little girl. I think I hated him for years. That hate kept me from seeing just how much you were struggling with your feelings over the whole thing. I'm sorry, Jack. I let you down. Please forgive me?"

Max opened his arms, and Jack fell into them. She wept uncontrollably, and only after several minutes did she hear her father's sounds of grief. Both had hurt for so long and hanging onto the hurt was almost destroying them.

"I still feel like it's all my fault," Jack's voice was barely audible. "I can't seem to get it out of my head that somehow, if I had done something, Grandpa would still be alive today."

"Jack," Max said gently, "Grandpa was on a fast track to the grave. He drank so much that it was literally killing him. Did you know that his own doctor had given him less than a year to live? His liver was shot. He'd destroyed it through his alcoholism."

"I didn't know that," Jack looked totally puzzled.

"I thought I mentioned it before...but it was such a crazy time. I held out hope, until the very end, that somehow he would come back to God and it would turn his life around." Max sighed loudly, as he ran a hand through his hair. "I used to dream of the old Grandpa. I used to dream that one day he'd return," he said looking at Jack sadly, "but it wasn't meant to be.

"I loved him, Jack. Before Grandma died, he was such a different person, such a good person. You know how everyone loved him. He could never deal with Grandma's death. He never got over it. He died with her that day."

As Max eased the truck back onto the road toward the Inn, he spoke urgently again. "Jack, don't marry Bradley because Grandpa liked him, or because Grandpa decided he was right for you. And," he put a hand on her shoulder, "don't go to

Africa unless you are confident in your heart that God is calling you to do so. That's too high a compromise. Life is too short, Jack. Live it for God and for God alone."

"How did you know about Africa?" Jack wondered aloud.

"I promised not to reveal my sources," Max winked at her, "but those sources are very worried about you. They spoke to me out of concern for you."

Jack nodded understandingly.

Max paused and then groaned quietly. "Jack," his voice was soft but urgent, "God is good, and God is faithful. In all your ways acknowledge Him, and He will direct your path. It's a promise we can count on."

Jack nodded, hugged her Dad, and slowly got out of the truck. She made her way down to the docks. As she studied the sky, she knew a storm was brewing. Despite her better judgment, she readied her cat to sail. She needed desperately to get away and think. She needed to escape.

A voice from behind her startled her and made her jump. "I hope you're not planning on going out." Matthew's voice held clear warning in it. "There's a storm coming."

Jack stared at him for a minute before she spoke. "Stay out of it, Matthew," she answered in an angry, stubborn tone. "I need to get away."

As Jack pushed her cat away from the dock, Flyer, as well as Matthew, jumped on board. Jack stared at her unwanted crewmembers with a mixture of anger and disbelief. "Get off my boat!" she commanded him. "I want to be alone!"

"If you're going out, then so am I." Matthew addressed her in such a determined way, Jack knew it was useless to argue with him.

Jack just stared at him angrily. She didn't want company, and she didn't want a babysitter.

"And," Matthew's tone was clear with warning, "don't you even dare try to dump me off your boat, Jack Miller. If I catch you doing so, I'll throw you overboard myself. I'm here to stay."

"I can see that," Jack mumbled angrily. "I can see that!"

Fifteen

As soon as Jack pulled the sail tight, her catamaran took off like a shot out of a gun. Matthew braced himself for the uncertainty that lay ahead. The sky was gray, the wind was blowing at a furious pace, and the lake was already covered in whitecaps.

It was a foolish time to go out sailing, Matthew thought shaking his head angrily, and it was an extremely foolish time to take a cat out on the lake. They were the most unstable boats he knew of. They rode the water on two pontoons, and although it made them incredibly quick, it also made them incredibly easy to tip over or flip altogether.

They were flying across the lake so fast that Matthew actually looked down to make sure they were touching the water. Hydroplaning seemed all too possible here. Jack had the left pontoon flying high out of the water, with her body hanging far off the side of the boat to balance it. Stupid was the word that continually came to his mind. Death or being seriously maimed were other thoughts that played around in his head. Nothing was comforting about this journey. Not a single thing. Even Flyer, who normally looked relaxed on the cat, was fully alert, with concern spread across his fuzzy face. Flyer didn't like the ride any more than he did.

Matthew looked to his right and noticed Bear Island rapidly approaching. He prayed that Jack would stop there. Bear Island had a safe harbor, and it would be better to ride the storm out there than in the middle of Eagle Lake.

A wave hit the boat hard and threw Flyer into Matthew's lap. The dog looked positively scared. At this moment the dog had more common sense than its master, and that fact alone did nothing to comfort Matthew at all.

"Hey, Jack," Matthew tried to sound calm, "where are your life jackets? I want to strap one on Flyer and me." He paused a moment, looking around for them. "You'd better put one on, too. We're in for a rough ride."

It was a minute before Jack answered. "I forgot to bring them," she shouted above the noise of the rising wind.

Matthew felt as if someone had hit him hard in the gut. What a stupid situation he had gotten himself into. Out on the lake in the middle of the worst storm he had ever seen without any life jackets and with a captain who had gone mad.

Hope surged through him as he saw Pine Tree Island quickly approaching. The way Jack was sailing, everything was quickly approaching and then swiftly vanishing. He felt as though he were sitting in a racecar. Unfortunately for him, the driver was no more stable than a bee whose hive had been knocked over.

"Why don't we stop at Pine Tree?" Matthew asked, trying to keep the fear out of his voice. He tried not to sound desperate, but the fear within him was barely being contained.

"I'm going to Blueberry," Jack shouted back to him against the wind.

Matthew's heart sank. They'd never make it. It was a full mile further down the lake. The way the wind and waves were increasing in power, the old cat was bound to flip over. It wasn't designed to be sailed in a storm.

He wasn't aware of the rain right away. At first he thought the water hitting his face was spray from the boat. As it began falling on him in steady sheets, he realized they would be cold and wet within seconds. Sarcastically, he thought it made little difference if they got wet. They were going to die, so what difference did it make if they died wet or dry?

Not more than a minute later, he truthfully admitted to himself that he did not wish to die.

"Please God," he prayed, as he had never prayed before, "please let us make it safely to shore. Keep us safe, and let us live."

Sometime, in the midst of his pleading to God, Jack turned slightly so she could face him. "Matthew, I'm sorry. I should have stopped at Pine Tree."

He felt like yelling at her, "You shouldn't have gone out sailing in a storm!" Instead he said, as calmly and as encouragingly as possible, "Blueberry Island is half a mile away. If you keep both pontoons in the water, we'll make it."

I hope we'll make it, he thought, feeling panicked. "Please, God, help us." Matthew's 911 prayers continued fervently.

Matthew watched with growing concern as Jack fought the wind, trying to keep both pontoons in the water. The wind was so strong that every time it gusted, the boat would go sideways instead of forward. It made the idea of getting to Blueberry Island seem like more of a dream than a reality.

Matthew's spirits began to rise when they rounded a corner and Blueberry Island came into view. He guessed they were about a quarter mile from it. "We can get to use that emergency shelter." Matthew struggled to add hope to a very dim situation.

Jack nodded as the wind gusts slammed her boat. Her left pontoon rose high in the air, and Matthew tightened his grip on Flyer as he braced for the inevitable flip. Jack quickly loosened the sail rope, to slow down the cat's speed. The wind decreased momentarily, and both pontoons fell back into the water again.

Matthew breathed a prayer of relief. As he held the shaking pup in his lap, his eyes caught sight of something shiny passing them in the water. As his panicked brain was trying to identify the shiny, gray material, another piece passed him in the water. Alarm slammed through his body as he recognized exactly what it was. It was the duct tape that was supposed to be holding the pontoons together. His panic skyrocketed to an entirely new level.

As he was trying to process all that was happening, he noticed that the front of the boat was starting to angle downward. Jack noticed it, too, and the look of panic that crossed her face did nothing to calm his own out-of-control emotions. They both had been sailing too long to pretend that they didn't know what was going to happen. They were going down. They were going to sink about a quarter mile off of Blueberry Island, in the middle of a raging storm.

"Just keep her on course, Jack!" Matthew shouted. "If we had to swim at this point, we could." Matthew knew that he was lying, and he hoped God wouldn't be mad at him for it. He wanted desperately to give Jack hope and confidence. It might just pull her through.

Stay positive, he kept telling himself. Yet in reality, there was very little to be positive about. They were going down in a storm. He knew he was a strong swimmer. Yet if he was being saddled with supporting a frightened dog as well as a scared woman through high waves, he feared none of them would make it to shore.

Fog was encompassing the borders of the lake and slowly moving in on them. Like a silent enemy preparing for an attack, its eerie quality only made the situation they were in seem even more desperate.

Matthew kept his eyes focused on the target ahead. Blueberry Island was getting closer. He noticed Jack was aiming her cat straight for it. Once again, alarm crashed through him. The angle that Jack was bringing the boat in on was going to drive them straight into the rocks on the island's south end.

"Jack," Matthew shouted, not caring if this time his voice revealed the panic he felt inside. He didn't have to finish his question. Jack knew where he was going.

"I can't harbor off Sandy Beach," Jack answered in a shaky tone. "I'll never make the turn into the bay. The boat is not only sinking, it's falling apart."

She was right. Matthew knew in an instant that she was right. He also felt that they were doomed.

"I'm aiming for the line between those rocks," Jack said as she stared straight ahead.

Line was a good description, Matthew thought fearfully. If Jack veered off course for more than a few feet either way, Captain Crunch would take them all to an early grave.

"It seems too risky," Matthew shouted back to her.

"Got any better ideas?" Jack asked anxiously. "If you do, I'd definitely like to hear them now. I don't see any good alternative."

Matthew quickly evaluated the situation and realized Jack was right. There was no better plan. The thought made him cringe inside.

"Have you ever tried to enter the island from this direction?" Matthew asked her anxiously.

"Never," Jack admitted quietly. Her voice was deadly serious. She had been sailing far too long not to know the danger they were in. "It would be crazy to enter from this direction. Even in good weather, the rocks make it too great of a danger."

As Matthew sat there being the self-appointed lookout man, his stomach clenched more tightly than it had before. The sky was gray, the water was dark...and the rain and wind in his direct line of vision made it close to impossible for him to accurately make out all of the rocks. Everywhere he looked there were rocks. Some were high above the water. Those you could see were no problem. The ones he was the most afraid of were the ones just below the surface of the water. Even on a clear day, it was hard to spot them. You didn't usually see them, you'd hear them as your boat scraped across the top of them. All the while you'd be praying that they didn't rip your boat apart like a can opener. It was an awful sound.

Neither one of them saw the rock that hit the old, beat-up right pontoon. They heard it as it threw them from the boat, through the air, and into the dark raging water. Matthew felt like he was jet-propelled into a boulder. His right side took the blow. He felt amazed that he was not only alive, but also able to move. His right side was scratched up and bleeding, but as he slowly began to move about, he felt confidant that nothing was broken. He might be bruised for life, but no bones were broken.

He instantly began to search for Jack. He scanned the rocky graveyard quickly, but couldn't find her. "God, no!" he screamed against the elements of the storm. "Help me find her!"

As he continued scanning the area back and forth, he saw a form that had been tossed upon a flattish rock. It reminded him of road kill. He fought against the water to make his way there. Every time he swam two strokes forward, he felt the storm grab him and push him back three strokes. This wasn't working.

"God, help me!" Matthew screamed out in desperation. "She's going to drown if I don't get to her." With a renewed sense of urgency, Matthew fought his way between the rocks. He made it to knee-deep water and could move a little quicker.

As he reached Jack, his worst fears were confirmed. She wasn't breathing, and from the look of the gash on her head, he knew she had hit the rock hard. Matthew sprang into action. He laid her flat on her back and quickly pulled her a few feet to the beach. He immediately started performing CPR on her. He talked out loud as he nervously went through each step. He wasn't sure how long into the procedure it was before Jack responded. She began vomiting up water. Matthew rolled her onto her side so she wouldn't choke. She gagged anyway, coughing and sputtering as the water came out of her. When things subsided, she collapsed on her back with a loud groan. She stayed awake just long enough to say three things. "Thank you. I'm sorry. Where's Flyer?" Then Jack passed out.

Matthew turned in time to see Flyer dragging himself out of the rough surf sputtering and choking. He looked half drowned and his right leg was tucked up underneath him. Matthew felt pretty sure the pup had broken it.

As soon as Flyer spotted Matthew, he immediately started hobbling over to him. Matthew felt very relieved to see the brave dog alive. Doing CPR on a person was one thing. Doing it on an animal was an entirely different story.

As Flyer collapsed next to him, Matthew gently patted him and spoke to him soothingly as he carefully examined him. Besides the obvious broken leg, Flyer seemed to be in decent shape.

"I'm sorry, Boy," Matthew tried to comfort the injured pup. "You're going to have to walk to the cabin. I've got to carry Jack."

He didn't know how a 5'5" man was supposed to carry a woman who was 5'8". As he made his way back to Jack, pieces of her boat started washing to shore. An idea struck him so hard that he felt it came from God Himself. If he could get the sail, or a piece of it, he could lay Jack on it and drag her the quarter mile or so to the cabin.

After he checked on Jack again, he went to the water's edge and searched frantically for the bright, rainbow-colored sail. He spotted it washing up on some rocks a few hundred yards away.

When he got to it, he grabbed a piece of the sail nearest him, and tugged. It was almost as though the water were tugging back. It seemed impossible to move. The sail, laden down with water, was not only slippery, but also extremely heavy.

Matthew waded out into the water and managed to surface enough of the sail so he could pull it free. He dragged the sail along the beach until he got to Jack.

Immediately he checked her pulse again and listened to her breathing. Both seemed fairly steady, especially considering what they'd just been through. He rolled Jack carefully onto the sail, and then began pulling her toward the cabin.

Matthew found that the rain was actually working for him. The path was slippery, and the footing was difficult, but the sleek sail slid easily over the muddy, pine-needle path.

As Matthew tugged Jack along the path, he couldn't help but be moved by the sight. The woman he loved was lying helplessly on a tarp, while her dog was limping painfully behind her. Matthew prayed for strength and wisdom to get them both through this.

When they finally reached the small log cabin, Matthew leaned Jack against him, and brought her inside the house. He laid her down on the pine floor, in front of the stone fireplace. After he checked her again, he went outside to the shed for wood. He was grateful the woodshed was well built, and the wood was dry.

Within ten minutes he had a small fire going. Flyer curled up right next to Jack in front of the blaze.

They both looked OK for the time being, so then he went in search of blankets. He found four thick army blankets in a cabinet and grabbed them all.

He removed Jack's wet sneakers and socks and carefully wrapped her in three blankets. Flyer, who had been forced to get up in this process, curled up against Jack as soon as he could. Even in pain and disaster, the dog was true and faithful to his master. Matthew lovingly stroked the dog's wet head.

Matthew was able to locate a first aid kit. He tried to clean up Jack's bleeding forehead as best as he could. He managed to secure a few butterfly bandages to her forehead, and that seemed to stop the bleeding for now.

With the situation under control, Matthew grabbed the fourth blanket, and dropped in a heap in front of the fireplace. He was so exhausted that he fell asleep before he knew it.

Matthew woke up some time later to the sound of low moaning. He rolled over and put a hand on Jack's shoulder, and she opened her eyes partially.

"How are you?" he asked in a concerned voice, as he observed his patient carefully.

"Head…" mumbled Jack.

"You cracked it open like an egg." Matthew's joke came out sounding lame to his own ears. The situation was still too serious for him.

"Arm…" Jack whispered in a voice that was alarming weak.

"Which one?" Matthew asked attentively. He hadn't noticed any injuries to her arms.

"Right," Jack answered him through clenched teeth.

Matthew unwrapped her blankets enough to see her right arm. It took only a quick survey of the arm to see that it had indeed been broken. The arm, from the elbow down, lay at a crooked, unnatural angle.

"It's broken," Matthew stated matter-of-factly. "Let me see if I can find something to splint it with. That will help some."

Matthew found a small flat piece of kindling wood and then searched the room for something to tie it to her arm with. As he walked around the small cabin, his shoe had become untied. As he stared down at his laces, an idea clicked, and a moment later he was pulling them from his sneakers.

"This will work," he said to himself as he walked back to Jack.

He set up the temporary splint, laying the wood against her arm and securing it with his sneaker laces. As he wrapped his patient up again, Jack mumbled something to him.

"What was that, Honey?" he leaned in closer to her.

"Radio."

"Where?" Matthew asked, instantly alert. This was their ticket out of here.

"Kitchen drawer..." It was all Jack had to say. Matthew took off for the kitchen as fast as his wobbly legs would carry him.

He found the radio and turned it on. To his great relief, it crackled to life. He would have to thank the Rangers for the great job they did stocking up the cabin. It probably had saved their lives.

"Anyone there?" he asked lamely into the radio. There was nothing. No response of any kind.

Matthew's heart sank some, but he immediately tried again. It was his only hope. "Helloooo...we need help here!" His voice came across in an unmistakably desperate tone.

"You've got Ranger Thompson at Eagle Lake Station," a calm voice answered his call. "Go ahead."

Matthew felt so relieved at the sound of someone's voice he began to cry. His whole body suddenly felt so weak, he thought he might collapse. He leaned against the kitchen counter for support. The ordeal had been so awful. It was the worst thing he had ever been through in his life. He had thought at least one or even all of them might die. Yet with God's grace, they had made it through. Now that he had made contact with the Ranger Station, it would only be a matter of time before help would be on the way. Hope surged through him. It was going to be OK. Everything was going to be OK.

Matthew forced himself to speak. In a choked-up voice he began, "This is Matthew Bishop. I'm at the emergency cabin on Blueberry Island."

"Go on, Matthew," the Ranger sounded attentive and alert.

"I'm here with Jack Miller. Her catamaran crashed against the rocks on the south end of the island."

"What is the condition of everyone?" the Ranger asked urgently.

"I'm fine," Matthew answered quickly, trying hard to control the shaking in his voice. He needed to get the facts out and try to be calm for Jack's sake.

"Jack Miller has been hurt badly. She has a severe concussion and a broken arm. There may be more, but that's all I could see."

"You're doing fine, Matthew," the Ranger assured him. "I will be landing a rescue helicopter with my team in five minutes in the clearing next to the cabin."

"Thank you, Sir." Matthew had been holding the radio so tightly that his hand hurt. It had been his lifeline to the outside world. He wanted to break down and sob, but he knew he had to keep it together for Jack. She needed him.

As he called over to Jack to tell her the news, alarm slammed through him when she didn't respond. As he got closer to her, he could tell that she had either passed out again, or fallen asleep.

He shook her lightly at first. When she didn't react, he shook her a little harder. Nothing. She was passed out. Matthew grabbed her wrist, and took her pulse. It wasn't as strong or as steady as before. While he continued to hold her wrist he noticed the shaking. At first he thought it was Jack. As he let go of her wrist, the shaking persisted. Not until that point did he realize he was shaking all over.

"Stupid nerves!" he scolded himself. "Get a grip!"

He stayed on the floor next to Jack and Flyer, listening for the helicopter. The first sound that grabbed him was the quiet. It was so quiet, it was deafening. He felt as though he could hear nothing. He couldn't take the quiet. He was so impatient for the helicopter to arrive, he got up and went to the window, willing the blasted machine to come quickly.

As he looked out the window, the first thing Matthew noticed was that the storm had ended. The wind and the rain had stopped completely. The sun was now breaking through the clouds, shining down upon the earth as if everything were normal.

"Amazing." Matthew felt astonished. "The only signs of the tragedy we've been through are our smashed-up bodies and Jack's bashed-up boat."

As Matthew got down on his knees to thank the Lord for bringing them through, he heard the sound he had been waiting for. It was the unmistakable sound of the blades of a helicopter slapping the sky. More tears formed. They were saved. Help was here.

As the chopper landed, two Ranger medics ran toward the cabin with a stretcher between them. Matthew opened the door and pointed toward where Jack lay on the floor.

Matthew stood by and watched closely as the medics examined Jack. After what seemed like an eternity, they slid Jack onto the stretcher. As they passed him, they asked if he could walk without help.

Matthew nodded.

"Then follow us. We'll send someone back to clean up the cabin."

"The dog?" Matthew asked anxiously. "We can't leave him."

Flyer stood up on his three good legs, looking uncertain as to what he should do.

"Bring him with you," the medic answered good-naturedly. "It looks like the poor dog could use some medical help."

As they were in the helicopter flying toward
Maine General Hospital, Matthew kept wondering
the same thing over and over. Exactly what was it
that got Jack so upset she'd sail off into an oncoming storm? Jack was a good captain. She knew the
rules of the lake, and followed them intelligently.
What had made her lose her head like this?

He somehow felt that the problem involved
Bradley. He didn't know how, but he knew in his
heart Bradley was behind Jack's irresponsible
actions. He would deal with him later. Right now, he
watched the woman he loved, unconscious on a
stretcher, and prayed that God would bring her back.

Sixteen

$\mathcal{A}$s Matthew quietly walked into the room, he couldn't take his eyes off the young woman lying in the bed. Jack's body looked so lifeless and perfectly still. He went over to the sterile-looking hospital bed and felt her pulse. The doctors had assured him that she'd be fine, but he still needed to feel the steady beating of her heart.

A moment later, Jack opened up her eyes, and they locked onto Matthew's. He slipped his hand from her wrist to her palm and held it tightly. He wanted to take her and gently rock her in his arms, but he knew that was impossible. For now, he'd have to settle for simply holding her hand.

"Thank you," Jack whispered emotionally.

Matthew slowly nodded his head. "There's no need to thank me, Jack."

"According to the Rangers, you saved my life."

"I'm glad I was there to help."

"Matthew, I owe you so much that I don't know where to start." Jack's voice had become so tight it was hard to talk.

Matthew wanted to get down on his knees and propose to her right then and there. The only thing that kept him from doing that was, as far as he knew, she was still an engaged to someone else. So, in a quiet, reassuring voice, he said kindly, "You don't owe me a thing, Jack."

They continued to stare at each other, unable to tear their eyes away. What they had between them had only grown more intense through the trauma they had survived. It had made them both realize how fragile life really was. It had also made them realize how special their relationship was. As they continued to gaze longingly into each other's eyes, a deep clearing of the throat brought them both reluctantly back down to earth.

"How are you feeling, Matthew?" Max asked, extending a warm hand to the young pastor.

"Fine, Sir," Matthew replied honestly. It felt so good to be with Jack again and know that she was going to be OK, that his legs could have been chopped off and he'd still have claimed he was fine. He smiled. Love does funny things to a person's heart and his outlook on life.

"I want to thank you for what you did for Jack." Max didn't attempt to hide the tears running down his face. "I'm so glad you were there. I fear I would have been attending her funeral about now, instead of visiting her in the hospital." Max glanced in Jack's direction, but not before Matthew got a clear view of the anguish that was covering his face. As her father, the last few hours must have been torturous. He couldn't imagine what Max had gone through after he found out Jack had taken her boat out in the storm. It must have been a nightmare for him.

As Max continued to look at his daughter, he thoughtfully asked her, "I'd be very interested in the reason you took your boat out in that storm. You're a first-rate sailor. You know better than that."

Before Jack could answer, her mother and sisters piled into the room in a wave of noise and confusion. "How are you, Dear?" her mother asked her, going over and giving her a careful hug. "You can't imagine how worried your father and I were."

"Jack!" Andy pushed her way through the people to the bedside. "I can't believe this! Are you OK? What happened?"

"She looks all right to me," Jay said angrily "and it's a good thing, because now I'm going to kill her! What in the world were you doing? You scared us to death!"

"Jack," Sam yelled excitedly, poking her head around the door, "look who came to visit!" A moment later she walked Flyer in, his leg in a cast and his tail wagging a million miles per hour.

218

"Flyer!" Jack shouted. "How did they smuggle you in here?" As Jack looked at Sam for the answer, her sister laughed.

"Trust me, you don't want to know."

"Can you lift him up on my bed?" Jack asked Matthew anxiously.

Matthew nodded, and carefully lifted the dog, cast and all, onto his owner's lap. Flyer's tail was going even faster than before as Jack's arms locked around his neck. She spoke soft words to him, and then buried her face in his soft coat and wept. Arms of love and support went around her and Flyer until her tears subsided.

"Jack," Max held his daughter's hand tenderly, "do you want to talk about it?"

"Not yet, Dad," Jack answered with a heavy heart. Max nodded understandingly.

"I bet it somehow involves that jerk Bradley." Jay grew heated. "Just say the word, Jack, and I'll pound him. You know I've wanted to knock his lights out for years."

"You'll have to stand in line for that." Ray sounded determined as he hobbled into the room. "Roy and I have got dibs on him first."

The old brothers shuffled over to the bedside and looked at Jack with tears in their eyes. "Sweetie," Roy addressed Jack gently, "Ray and I feel so responsible for what happened here."

"Why?" Jack asked, perplexed.

"We gave you the information that led to the fight."

"It was not either of your faults," Jack spoke sincerely, from her heart. "And," Jack smiled at her longtime friends, "for the record, Bradley and I didn't have a fight. We had a discussion."

Roy and Ray exchanged a knowing smile. "That's not what we heard." Roy had a distinct twinkle in his eye. "According to old Hank Webber, you threw Bradley, along with his lunch, off the town dock." Roy laughed at the thought. "Gee, Jack, if I knew you were going to do that, I'd have gotten ringside seats to the event!"

Jack had to laugh. It must have made quite a scene, and poor Bradley hated a scene. As she looked around the room, she had to laugh again at the startled expressions on her sisters' faces, as well as Matthew's.

"I think we're missing a few details here, Jack." Andy threw her hands on her hips. "What exactly happened between you two?"

"I don't want to talk about it right now," Jack grew serious.

Roy laughed loudly. "I just bet you don't, Honey!"

"Well, in my opinion, not that anyone in this family ever listens to it," Jay spoke adamantly, "you should have pushed that bum off the dock years ago!"

"Where is the big chicken?" Andy scanned around the room. She appeared ready to take him on right now.

"Told him not to come," Roy said quietly, but firmly. "I told him this was a place for family."

"Yup, and he isn't family yet," Ray added angrily.

"We should let Jack rest." Max's voice was full of fatherly concern. "I'm sure she's got a whopper of a headache."

Jack closed her eyes for a minute. "I feel like my head's been run over by a truck," she admitted in a pained voice.

"I hope you got some sense knocked into that thick head of yours concerning Bradley," Jay said hotly. "If this didn't do it, nothing will!"

"Jayme!" Max reprimanded her firmly. "It's time to leave!"

Jay stared at her father wide-eyed. He had only called her Jayme a handful of times in her entire life. Each time he did, she knew she was in hot water.

As the Miller clan filed out of the room, Jack's mother promised to be back soon to stay the night. She was determined to take care of her daughter. Jack couldn't miss the tears in her mother's eyes. She felt awful for what she had put her family through. She determined to talk to them the next day and ask their forgiveness.

As Matthew was passing by her bed on the way out, she took his hand and asked him to stay a moment. He agreed right away, and also agreed to take Flyer home later so Jack could spend a little more time with her dog.

"I wanted to talk to you first," Jack said slowly to Matthew. "I wanted to talk to you in private, without the entire family here."

Matthew nodded and pulled a chair up near the side of the bed. He sat patiently waiting until she was ready to speak. He glanced at Flyer and smiled. The dog had made himself so comfortable on Jack's bed that he was snoring quietly.

"I want you to know what happened." Jack's quiet voice trailed off. "I want you to understand why I did what I did."

Matthew nodded compassionately. "If you feel up to it, Jack."

Jack looked at him seriously. "I lost my head. I was so angry at Bradley that I lost all my judgment." Jack sighed loudly, and Flyer lifted his head to look at her. She patted his head reassuringly, and he curled back up.

"I knew something was seriously wrong." Jack closed her eyes wearily. A second later she popped them back open and smiled. "My informants, Roy and Ray, overheard Bradley's phone conversation but wouldn't give me the details."

"How?" Matthew asked curiously.

Jack laughed. "They hide in the central hall closet when people are using the hall phone."

Matthew's mouth dropped open in shock. "Please tell me you're kidding."

"It's no joke." Jack laughed again. "Dad's been trying to get them to stop it for years. It's nearly impossible, because they're always around the house, and they're downright sneaky!"

"I can't believe what I'm hearing!" Matthew's face was flooded in shock.

"I don't think I'll ever use that phone again."

Jack smiled at him. "If you're planning on having a private conversation, I wouldn't recommend it. You really never know when they're hiding in there."

"They need a hobby," Matthew said shaking his head.

"Unfortunately for us," Jack smiled again, "that is their hobby. Consider yourself forewarned."

"Thanks for the tip," Matthew winked at her. "I just wish you had told me a few months ago."

Jack paused for a minute, and her face grew serious again. "Anyway, I confronted Bradley. I told him I knew something was up, and I demanded that he tell me what it was."

"Was that before or after you tossed him in the lake?" Matthew asked with a twinkle in his eye.

"Before," Jack answered smiling at him. "I tend to get angry when I know I've been manipulated."

They both laughed, but Jack quickly grew serious again. "Do you know what he did?"

Matthew shook his head no.

"He signed us up for a five-year missions trip to Africa," Jack explained in an exasperated tone.

"He did what?" Matthew's mouth dropped open in disbelief.

"Five years..." Jack closed her eyes. "Africa."

"You don't have to go," Matthew said adamantly, sounding like a tough defense lawyer.

Jack smiled at him. "I don't intend to." She released a loud sigh. "I know God's calling for me is in Sugar Creek. I just wish Bradley had discussed this with me first."

"He probably knew that you'd say no." Matthew was angry.

Jack laughed. "No kidding I would have said no. I'm scared to death of the jungle. I'm positively terrified of spiders and snakes, and I get poison ivy in places I can't even talk about!"

Matthew smiled at her last comment. "He probably thought he could talk you into it."

"Knowing Bradley, he probably did, and on top of it all," Jack closed her eyes again, "his reasons for going were all wrong. He thought going to

Africa would look good on his resume. He felt that it would get him a job at a large church."

Matthew's face fell. "That's really awful. I don't even know what to say."

Jack smiled. "You don't have to say anything."

"So what's going to happen now?" Matthew asked her in a concerned tone. "Are you going to wait for him to return from Africa?"

"No." Jack's answer was quiet, but determined. "The good thing about all this is that I have finally seen the light."

"Oh?" Matthew inched closer to her. "Would you care to explain?"

Jack smiled at him. "I thought you might be especially interested in this part."

"I think so." Matthew smiled charmingly.

"God has freed my heart from the guilt that I felt about losing my grandfather. You and my dad and my sisters were right, Matthew." Jack paused, closing her eyes tightly. "The only reason I was marrying Bradley was because of guilt. I felt so guilty that I was at the wheel when my grandpa died. I thought the least I could do was honor his wish for me in this area. Somehow, I thought if I went through with the wedding, it would make everything all right. I thought it would ease my conscience."

Matthew looked at her so tenderly that she thought she was going to cry. "It doesn't work that way, Jack."

"I finally figured that out. As the wedding day was growing closer, I just felt worse. I don't love Bradley at all." Jack patted Flyer gently. "Right now, I'm not even sure I like him."

Matthew took her hand and held it lovingly. "When are you going to tell him?"

"Tomorrow," Jack said with conviction. "I want you to ask him to come by the hospital tomorrow morning. Can you do that for me?"

"Yes," Matthew nodded seriously. "I think I'll plan to come by tomorrow afternoon." A huge smile spread over his face. "You and I have a lot of things to talk about. First you need to bring closure to your relationship with Bradley," Matthew said thoughtfully. "Then," he looked at her so tenderly she could scarcely breathe, "you and I need to have a nice long talk."

"You think so?" Jack asked, lost in the love she saw in his eyes.

"I know so," Matthew admitted as he affectionately held her eyes with his own. Reluctantly he got up and carefully lifted Flyer off her bed. As he turned to leave, he said lovingly, "There's so much I've been wanting to say to you. I've been holding things in for so long." He paused and sighed deeply. "I will be praying for your talk with Bradley and praying for my talk with you." Jack nodded, and then he was gone.

Seventeen

$\mathcal{T}$he next morning, as soon as visitors were allowed, Bradley strolled confidently into Jack's room carrying a large bouquet of wildflowers. "So, how's My Lady doing?" he asked her in a loud, cheerful tone.

Jack stared at him a minute through narrowed eyes while she tired to ignore her pounding headache. He acted like everything between them was completely fine. In a quiet voice, she answered him slowly. "I'll live, but I think I'm going to have a major headache for a while."

Bradley nodded thoughtfully, and then handed Jack the flowers. "I'm sorry about your boat, Jacilyn. It's got to be hard to lose her after all this time."

Jack felt choked up at the thought of losing her cat. She didn't want to think of her beloved boat smashed to pieces on the rocks at Blueberry Island. "I was so stupid to take her out with a storm coming. I feel fortunate that no one was permanently hurt."

Again, Bradley nodded solemnly. "Oh," he waved a hand at her as though a thought just popped into his head, "don't worry about Vacation

Bible School." He paused and grabbed a chair and pulled it close to her bedside. "Matthew is covering our class so I could come and see you."

Jack nodded as she looked at the flowers. They were beautiful, yet she couldn't appreciate them at the moment. Her mind was too absorbed with the matters she had to discuss with Bradley.

"I need to talk to you." Bradley pinned her with his eyes.

Jack nodded, and looked at him seriously. "I need to talk to you, too."

"Do you want to go first?" he asked her with just a trace of hopefulness in his voice.

Jack shook her head. "I think it would be better if you did."

"OK, then." The reluctance in his voice was obvious. He got out of his chair slowly and anxiously paced the room for a minute. Jack watched him curiously as he repeatedly ran a nervous-looking hand through his short blonde hair.

"Jacilyn," Bradley began in a quiet yet urgent tone, "I was wrong about the Africa trip. I should have discussed it with you first. I knew you'd say no, that's why I didn't."

"I'm not going to Africa," Jack was emphatic.

"Is there absolutely no chance that you'll change your mind?" Bradley asked in a hopeful voice. "I mean," he hesitated, "I want you to really think about this. Pray about this."

Jack shook her head angrily. The boy simply didn't get it. He had always manipulated her, and from the smug, confident expression on his strong face, he thought he could do it once again.

"Well," Bradley appeared certain of himself, "I have something here that just may help."

He walked to the side of her bed and handed her a small black velvet box that was distinctly from a jeweler. Jack's heart sank. There was little doubt in her mind as to what was inside. This was going to be harder than she thought. She didn't love Bradley, but she didn't want to hurt him, either.

"What is it?" she asked as she held the small box at a distance, as though she feared it might blow up.

Bradley stated in a sure voice, "Open it up, Silly. It's something that you should have had a long time ago."

Jack opened the box hesitantly, yet to her surprise she wasn't certain what was in it. It was a gold ring, that she was positive of, but she had expected an engagement ring. She thought she would be looking at a classic, traditional gold band—with a diamond. This ring had the gold band, and in the center there might have been something, but she honestly wasn't sure. After closer inspection, whatever was in the center of the ring was so small that she couldn't tell what it was.

Jack looked over at Bradley for an explanation, and a self-important smile spread across his face. "It's an engagement ring!" he stated as proudly as if he had given her the royal crown jewels themselves. "I picked it up yesterday," he added, as he studied the ring, apparently well pleased with himself.

Jack continued to stare at the ring as though she were in deep thought. Actually, she was in shock. What she was looking at was the cheapest excuse for an engagement ring that she had ever seen in her life.

"There's no diamond." Jack was completely stunned. She was positively flabbergasted.

"That's what I originally thought." Bradley leaned over to take a closer look at the stone. "You see," he pointed out in an excited, directing voice, "if you angle the ring this way, toward the light, there's a slight shine in the center. And that," Bradley announced proudly, "is the stone!"

Jack didn't know whether she was going to laugh or cry. It seemed to her that Bradley had spent more money on the flowers than on the ring. Not that the size of the stone mattered, she simply wanted a stone that you could see without putting a magnifying glass up to it.

Jack shut her eyes for a minute, trying to bring balance to her spinning world. Bradley tended to be cheap with gifts in the past, but this diamondless engagement ring took the cake. The thing that bothered Jack even more was the way that Bradley had no trouble whatsoever with spending money generously on himself. He was always decked out in expensive, trendy clothes from Maine's exclusive preppy shops. Why couldn't he, for once, spend a little money on her? For instance, having the jeweler put an actual diamond on the ring would have been nice for starters. Even a piece of glass would have been better than this. This ring would be embarrassing to wear. It wasn't worth a dime, and that's exactly how it made Jack feel. Worthless.

Jack slowly shut the box. She closed her eyes again and prayed that God would give her the words to say. She wanted Bradley to understand exactly how she felt. Breaking up with him was not because of Africa, or a diamondless engagement ring. It was for the sole reason that she didn't love him.

"Not feeling well?" Bradley asked casually. "Maybe I should have waited to give you such a special gift."

Jack slowly shook her head. "I can't marry you." She spoke softly but with deep conviction.

"What?" Bradley asked in shock, leaning closer to her. "What did you say?"

Jack turned her head to look directly into Bradley's eyes. How did she ever let Grandpa rope her into this, she thought disgustedly. "I can't marry you, Bradley," Jack's voice was a little louder this time.

Bradley lost his air of confidence immediately. He looked absolutely stunned. His mouth swung open and wiggled a little like a fish out of water, but no words came out.

"I'm sorry," Jack said honestly. "I shouldn't have let things go on for so long." She placed the velvet box back in Bradley's hands, and he just stared at it completely speechless. He looked so baffled that Jack actually felt sorry for him. Clearly this proud man was not used to rejection.

Finally, a small quiet word escaped Bradley's lips. "Why?" he asked in a puzzled tone.

"I don't love you," Jack admitted seriously.

"You don't…" He couldn't bring himself to say any more. He acted like a man lost in a deep fog. He was grasping out for anything to hold on to, yet he kept coming up empty each time. He was trying hard to connect all the dots here, but it just wasn't making sense to him.

"I'm sorry." Jack's words came from the bottom of her heart. She didn't want to hurt him, but she knew, now more then ever, she didn't want to marry him either.

Bradley began pacing the room again. He looked like a wild animal that had been caged. "Me..." Bradley pointed his finger to his chest. "You don't love ME!" He honestly had trouble comprehending the idea.

Jack shook her head slowly. "No," she answered slowly but decisively.

Bradley continued to pace. "It's about that Africa thing, isn't it?" he snapped his fingers together. "You're just mad at me."

From the smug expression on his face, Jack could see that he thought he had solved the puzzle. He looked completely regal again. His composure was back in full, and he crossed his arms and stared at Jack confidently. "I'm right, aren't I?" he asked in a self-satisfied way.

Jack almost burst out laughing. She bit the inside of her lip to try to help contain it. The man was positively pretentious. "No, Bradley," Jack replied candidly, "I never loved you. I feel it's wrong to marry someone that I don't love."

He shook his head in disbelief. "Never?" he asked in astonishment.

Jack slowly shook her head. She was starting to wish she had written him a note. She watched anxiously as Bradley started to pace again.

"How can that be?" he asked, spreading his arms open wide. "We have been together for so long." He pinned her with a stare, and asked directly, "Never, ever? You never, ever loved me?"

"No." Jack shook her head slowly. "Grandpa wanted me to marry you and when he died, I felt obligated to fulfill his plan."

"OK," Bradley appeared thoughtful as he nodded his head up and down. "I'm OK with that, Jacilyn. I still want to marry you. I believe in time you will come to love me."

This time Jack's mouth dropped open. She couldn't believe what she was hearing. "Bradley," she was clearly flustered by the turn of events, "we have known each other since we were eight. That's fifteen years!" Jack paused and sighed loudly. "If I have not fallen in love with you in fifteen years, I seriously doubt I ever will. You and I are two very different people, wanting very different things out of life. We're not meant for each other. That's clear to me now. And, I have come to realize that although our marriage was Grandpa's plan, it is not God's plan."

Bradley sighed loudly. His tearful eyes just continued to evaluate her. "So, that's the way it's going to be then, is it? There's nothing I can do or say to make you want me?"

"No," Jack answered firmly. "It's no way to go into a marriage."

Bradley gazed at her longingly, but nodded in agreement. "I know that I'm a mess, Jacilyn. I've struggled with my priorities for as long as I can remember. I'm going to try to straighten myself out. I realize it's too late for us. I always knew in my heart that you deserved better. You have a depth to you, and a genuine honesty that I rarely see in people today. You're special, and you should marry someone equally special."

He paused, took his jeweler's box and flowers back, and then said in a sad voice, "Thanks for staying with me for as long as you did. You're the best thing that ever happened to me, and I'm sorry I wasn't the same for you."

As he turned to go, Jack asked him in a concerned voice what he was going to do.

"I'm going to Africa," Bradley stated in a miserable, hollow voice.

"Really?" Jack asked in surprise.

"It still seems like a good idea to me." He paused, took one long last look at her, and then said quietly, "See you in five years."

Jack stared at the door long after Bradley had left. The sadness she felt almost swallowed her up. How awful to know the truth of God and choose directly not follow it. Bradley was going to Africa on his own strength, with his own agenda in mind. Jack slowly shook her head. In her heart, she wondered if Bradley would ever change. Even though he was now officially a pastor, she couldn't help but wonder if he would ever really trust God, and live his life for Him.

Eighteen

To Jack's surprise and enormous pleasure, her doctor came in later that morning and released her. She was thrilled to be going home. She never slept well at the hospital and greatly looked forward to the peace and quiet of the lake.

After two days of being confined to a bed, Jack insisted she was going to stay outside for a while. Her father set up a lounge chair on the south side of the boathouse to give her some privacy from the Inn's guests.

Jack dropped into her chair gratefully. Her head still ached, but her heart felt so free. For the first time in years, her heart honestly felt free. She never fully realized until now what her decision to stay with Bradley had cost her. It had cost her sweet freedom and peace, not to mention blocking God's plan for her life.

She thought about God's perfect plan for her throughout the morning hours as she absentmindedly watched the activity on the lake. The lake ferry was giving tours; people were skiing, swimming, fishing, and sailing. The world was alive, and Jack felt thankful to be part of it.

Her sisters came by throughout the morning to check on her and visit with her. Andy and Nicholas were the first ones to come by. Nicholas had scribbled an art original for her. Jack studied the picture for a moment and then smiled at her young nephew. "Tell me about it, Sweetie."

"New boat for Auntie. Bad boat gone. New boat good," Nicholas proudly pointed at the picture with his pudgy little hand.

Andy talked with Jack for a few more minutes before she left. The Inn was full of guests, and there was plenty of baking for her to do.

Jay came by next with some chocolate chip cookies and a letter that she gently placed in Jack's lap. It was addressed to Jay and Jack Miller.

"I believe you'll find it very interesting." Jay smiled as she reached out to grab a cookie.

Jack noticed the return address, and stared back at her sister in shock. "Ken and Cody Brady actually wrote us? I don't believe it!"

Jay nodded and laughed. "Yup, and wait until you see what they have to say!"

Jack quickly opened the letter and anxiously read. At first, the letter was all small talk. Updates on the weather, summer activities, crimes committed, and punishments they had to endure because of those crimes. Jack had to laugh at that.

Then the boys went on to describe their ride home. They had told their parents about what Jay and Jack had said about asking Jesus into their hearts. The boys went on to say that their mother said that she had asked Jesus into her heart as a child. The boys said they talked about Jesus all the way home. By the time they reached their home, Ken and Cody had both accepted Jesus. They and their mother were very excited about this.

The boys asked Jay and Jack to pray for their father. He said he was not interested in religion, but if it helped keep Ken and Cody out of trouble, he was glad.

As Jack finished reading the letter, tears were spilling out of her eyes. She looked over at Jay and saw her tough sister struggling to hold her own tears back. "God used us, Jay." Jack's voice was all choked-up. "God took a situation that was normally a disaster, and turned it around for the good."

Jay nodded thoughtfully. "I never thought I'd be saying this, but I actually came to care a great deal about those two little imps! I think we should write them back soon."

Jack nodded. "I miss them, too."

As the girls stared off over the lake, they were both lost in their own thoughts. God had used them. There were no words to describe the feeling of awe and privilege they felt when the God of the universe reached down to use two simple people. What an honor it was to be a part of His plan.

A few minutes later, Mail Boat Eddie went by and tooted his horn. As the girls watched him dock on the other side of the boathouse, Jack asked Jay about Eddie. "Do you think he and Sam will get married?"

Jay smiled thoughtfully. "I hope so. I think that they are made for each other."

Jack smiled and nodded in agreement.

"What about you and Bradley?" Jay asked seriously.

"Well," Jack paused, "you'll be glad to hear that I broke up with him this morning."

Jay looked closely at her sister to determine whether she was serious or joking. "You are serious." Her tone was disbelieving. "I never thought I'd live to see the day this happened."

Jack smiled. "Yes, I'm serious. I feel so good about the decision."

"Well, now I know for sure that miracles do happen." Jay slapped her knee. "I can't tell you how many years I have prayed about this. I'm sure God was sick of hearing about it." She paused and looked at her little sister seriously. "I knew Bradley was all wrong for you right from the start. Not to mention he's one of the most annoying people I've ever met. Do you have any idea how frustrating it was to watch the two of you? It was awful! You made me crazy!"

"I'm sorry for what I put you through." Jack paused and cleared her throat. "What I put myself through wasn't exactly a picnic either." She sighed loudly. "Thanks for all your prayers, Jay. I love you."

"You're welcome, and I love you, too, Sis," Jay bent down and gave her little sister a hug. "But I still think I should get some kind of a Nobel Peace Prize or something."

Jack laughed loudly. "You? A peace prize? You've got to be kidding!"

"Do you have any idea how many times I personally wanted to kill that self-righteous boyfriend of yours?" Jay asked with anger rising in her voice. "He was the worst! I consider myself peaceful for not pounding him into oblivion."

"I'm really sorry," Jack said honestly. "I was all messed up because of Grandpa."

"I know," Jay nodded understandingly. "And that only made it harder for me." Jay blew out a loud frustrated breath. "I felt the bug-headed boyfriend was just taking advantage of you."

"I wish I could be half as outspoken as you, Jay. You always have the courage and boldness to speak what's on your mind. I admire you greatly for that."

Jay laughed. "Don't admire me too much. My courage and boldness have gotten me into hot water plenty of times. It works against you, too."

"Yes," Jack agreed, "but you're honest, Jay. You don't play games with people. And," Jack turned and looked at her directly, "you're usually right in your opinions. It's just that people aren't always interested in what's right."

"Thanks, Jack." Jay's voice was tight with emotion. "Coming from you, that means a lot."

The sisters sat quietly, deep in their thoughts. So much had happened in the last few days, it was hard to take in.

"Oh," Jay said suddenly, "Mom wanted me to tell you that Matthew called."

"Oh?" Jack asked, suddenly very alert.

"Yes," Jay smiled at her. "It seems that the pastor is coming to visit you this afternoon. By the way," she looked at her sister thoughtfully, "are you ever going to let Matthew teach you to drive again? He'd be the perfect one to do it, you know."

"I've given that a lot of thought, Jay. I think I'm ready now to start driving again. I want to be a mom some day and drive around a van-load of kids."

"Anyone's kids in particular?" Jay asked with a huge smile planted on her face.

"Don't read too much into this, Jay," Jack grew a bit nervous. "Let's just take one thing at a time."

"Hey," Jay said as she got up to head back to the Inn, "this is one guy that I do approve of for you. You've got my blessing, and I'm staying out of it."

Jack looked up at her sister skeptically. "You think you can honestly stay out of my business? You've been throwing yourself into it since I was born. You were my own, self-appointed body-guard."

"I'll stay out of it," Jay answered seriously. "Just don't you mess things up! He's the perfect guy for you, Jack."

The sisters' eyes met for a moment. "He's the one, Jack," Jay said earnestly. "Trust Matthew, Jack. He's the one for you."

"Thanks," Jack said softly.

"You're welcome." As Jay quietly began heading toward the path, she paused and turned back to face her sister again. "I may charge you a 'finder's fee,'" she added jokingly. "I found him, and I knew that he'd be perfect for you!"

Nineteen

*M*atthew found Jack later that afternoon, still hidden on the other side of the boathouse. "How are you?" he asked her in a concerned voice as he approached her.

"Free." Jack smiled. " I'm free, Matthew. I can't remember when my heart has felt so free."

Matthew smiled tenderly at her as he sat down on the wooden dock beside her. "The truth will set you free," he whispered softly.

"Boy, is that right," Jack agreed knowingly. "I never realized what a weight I was carrying around until I let go of it." Jack paused for a minute, considering the words she said just spoken. "I feel like the weight of the world has been lifted off my shoulders."

"It's much better to let God carry the burdens." Matthew gazed across the lake. "When we carry them, they wipe us out physically and spiritually. Not to mention," Matthew added thoughtfully, "that we're not trusting God or allowing faith to work."

"True," Jack admitted softly as she closed her eyes for a minute.

"So tell me," Matthew asked curiously, "how did Bradley take the news?"

"He was surprised," Jack grew serious. "I really don't think he ever had a clue as to how I felt."

"I knew how you felt about him the first time I met you both," Matthew smiled at her.

Jack smiled back at him. "I knew you did, and that only made me feel extremely uncomfortable. You forced me to confront issues that I had buried." She paused a minute, and then said straight from her heart, "Thank you."

Matthew looked at her so lovingly that she had to turn away. He possessed a tenderness, love, and compassion that Jack had never seen in anyone before. It was intense and personal, and beyond any depth of caring she had ever known. Jack felt herself drawn to Matthew by an enticing, all-consuming, heartfelt connection. It was completely beyond words. It was a powerful attraction that pulled them together a little more each time they were around each other. It was simply irresistible. Matthew had a magnetic pull on her heart that just lured her closer to him. The grip was superhuman. She couldn't get enough of him.

"I have things I want to discuss with you, Young Lady." Matthew spoke lovingly. "Do you feel up to a serious talk?"

As Jack looked at Matthew, a huge smile spread across her face. "I think it's a good idea that we talk," she said warmly.

"I haven't been able to stop thinking about you since the day we met," Matthew said as he picked up Jack's hand and held it gently. "Do you have any idea how difficult it is for me to preach on Sundays from the pulpit, when the girl I love is sitting in the front pew looking like an absolute angel?"

Jack laughed cheerfully. "Why don't you tell me about it?"

Matthew laughed softly and touched the tip of her nose quickly. "I think I will. God and I have had more talks about you these past five months. I felt so guilty being in love with another man's fiancée. And," Matthew laughed loudly this time, "if you think there was ever a time I wanted to marry you two, you're crazy! What a situation I was in. I was the pastor that was supposed to marry the girl I love off to another guy."

He paused and then sighed deeply. "Not to mention the fact that you two were all wrong for each other. It was awful! The whole situation was terrible. So," Matthew sighed, raising his eyebrows, "I did a lot of praying. I kept begging God to take away the feelings that I had for you. He didn't, and my feelings only increased each time I saw you.

The more I got to know you, the deeper in love I fell with you."

"That's quite a problem," Jack teased the young pastor.

"It sure was, Funny Girl!" Matthew tweaked the tip of her nose again.

"Did you know," Matthew sounded frustrated, "that there were times when I would see you and Bradley together and feel so angry at the disrespectful way he was treating you, that I actually wanted to punch him in the nose?"

"You'd have to get in line." Jack shook her head. "Jay was on the verge of clobbering Bradley most of the time." Jack paused, and then continued slowly. "It was hard on me, too. I found myself instantly attracted to you, in a way that I'd never been attracted to anyone before. You're special, Matthew," Jack smiled lovingly. "I don't know anyone like you."

"Well, I think you're very special, too." Matthew let go of Jack's hand and started to get up. "In fact," Matthew's tone became light and playful, "you're so special that I brought you a present."

"Really?" Jack asked excitedly.

"Yup. Hang on. I hid it back here."

He went around the side of the boathouse, and came back in a second with a dozen long stemmed red roses in his arms. "These are for you." He looked at her so lovingly it overwhelmed her.

"Thank you!" Jack replied breathlessly. "I've never gotten a dozen roses before!"

"What?" Matthew asked in a confused tone. "What do you mean? Didn't you ever get roses from Bradley?"

Jack shook her head.

"How long did you two date? I mean," Matthew said angrily, "in all the time you were with him, the guy never brought you roses? No, wait," Matthew suddenly stopped. "This is our time. I don't want to get into that right now. This is our time, and Bradley is not invited."

Jack laughed. "That sounds good." She buried her face in the soft, velvety roses and drank in their fragrant scent. "These are so beautiful. Thank you!"

"You're welcome." Matthew knelt down next to her. "I wanted to give you roses the first time I told you I love you."

Jack's eyes flew up from the flowers and connected directly with Matthew's. "I love you, Jack Miller." He settled the roses down in her lap so he could hold her hands. "I love you with all my heart."

Jack's eyes filled with tears. "Matthew, you make me feel so cherished. I've never felt like this before."

"It's easy for me to cherish you, Jack. I love you." His words were spoken from the bottom of his heart.

"I love you, too, Matthew," Jack squeaked, all choked up. "The first time I saw you up at the pulpit, I knew I was in big trouble. I knew I loved you like I've never loved anyone before."

"And you waited five months to tell me!" Matthew acted exasperated.

"There were a few complications," Jack admitted honestly.

Matthew smiled broadly. "I'm aware of them."

As their eyes held each other's, Matthew leaned over and did something that he had been longing to do for months. He kissed the woman he loved. He kissed her softly and tenderly until his head swam with dizziness.

"Jack," Matthew's tone grew husky, as he pulled away from her reluctantly, "we need to talk." He sighed as he ran his hand through his short brown hair. "I need to talk to you before I'm so far gone that I can't think straight at all."

Jack smiled understandingly. "That sounds good to me."

Matthew pulled a jeweler's box from his pocket and handed it to Jack.

"More gifts?" She asked him with surprise written on her face.

Matthew smiled. "Open it," he urged her softly.

Jack opened it and saw a gorgeous sapphire ring. "It's beautiful!" She said in a breathless voice. "Blue is my favorite color."

Matthew smiled and nodded, as he gently put a hand on her cheek. "I know."

He took his hand away reluctantly, and thoughtfully looked out across the lake. "Jack," he said lovingly as he knelt down next to her, "I want to start courting you. Do you understand what that means?"

"How is it different from dating?" Jack asked him seriously.

"For me," Matthew began tenderly, "I would only court someone I intended to marry." Matthew paused, and took Jack's hands gently in his own. "This is a serious commitment, Jack. If you don't think you're ready for it, then you need to tell me."

Jack smiled broadly at Matthew and then studied the ring in her hand. "This is a dream-come-true, Matthew. I thought I had to marry Bradley, and that you would never be mine." Jack paused, and looked at Matthew lovingly. "I am ready for a serious commitment. I would marry you in a second if you asked me."

"Really?" A mixture of shock and excitement paraded across the young pastor's face. "Here, you'd better put this ring on your right hand, then, because I have another ring for your left hand."

Jack's eyes widened in surprise, as her heart surged with joy.

"Jack," Matthew began in a choked-up voice," I've asked your parents for permission to marry you, and they have given their blessing."

Jack couldn't contain her smile. "You've been a busy boy."

"Very," Matthew nodded. "This is about to be the shortest courtship in history." Matthew smiled at Jack affectionately.

"Jack," Matthew bent down on one knee, "I love you with all my heart. Will you marry me?"

Both their eyes filled with tears. Matthew handed Jack a beautiful engagement ring. It was traditional in style, and she smiled when she looked at the stone. It was perfect in size. Not so big that she felt awkward about it but plenty big enough to see it clearly.

"Yes," Jack said quietly, but her words were certain. "I will marry you. I love you, Matthew Bishop."

Matthew gently slid the diamond ring on Jack's left hand. Then he took Jack in his arms and held her lovingly. Jack had never felt more cherished in her life.

"Jack," Matthew whispered softly in her ear, "I'm not rushing things too much, am I? If I am, just say the word."

Jack leaned out of the embrace to look Matthew directly in the eye. "I think, considering the way we're feeling toward each other, that if we don't get married soon, we may be faced with too many physical temptations." Jack paused for a moment. "I love you, Matthew, with all my heart. I think it's best if we get married soon."

Matthew smiled, and nodded understandingly. "I agree, Sweetheart." He leaned in and kissed her again. "Let's go talk to your parents about scheduling a wedding. I think the sooner the better."

Jack couldn't have agreed with him more. He was her Prince Charming. He was her Knight in Shining Armor. He was her best friend, and the love of her life. He was the one. She had always known it in her heart. It was something she had no doubt about. The love between them was so strong, the connection coming straight from the heart.

She wanted to start her new life with Matthew as soon as possible. They would get married and in time start a family. She wanted to be by Matthew's side through thick and thin. She wanted to support him, and encourage him, and go through life with him by her side. She was in the deepest type of love with this wonderful man. It was a love that would carry them through the good times as well as the bad. It was a love that Jack knew would grow deeper all their lives.

This was just the beginning. It was just the starting line. She was about to begin one of life's greatest journeys with a man custom-designed for her. He was, after all, God's perfect choice for her. She knew in her heart that she could never settle for anything less than God's perfect choice for her. As her eyes looked into Matthew's again, her heart soared. She couldn't help but agree with God on how perfect he really was.

Stony Brook Farm

A New England Novel

Sharon Snow Sirois

Available Fall 2002

at

Your Local Bookstore

Stony Brook Farm

When Annie Smith attends a concert given by popular Christian singer Ryan Jones, all she could do was stare at him. The man standing before her was drop dead gorgeous, but it wasn't his appearance that had Annie stalled in her tracks. The man before her, that she was so carefully inspecting, closely resembled her husband that she had buried two years earlier. The similarities were not only amazing, they were down right alarming.

Annie soon discovers that Ryan Jones has much more in common with her late husband then just his appearance. When they meet, Annie feels an immediate, unexplainable attraction to Ryan. When the simple touch of their hands in greeting cause an emotional explosion in both of them, Annie feels confused and completely thrown off balance. For a moment, time stood still. The secret was out in the open. A man and woman, on the brink of something that neither anticipated but both understood. There was a connection of their hearts that couldn't be denied.

Stony Brook Farm

From Annie's Stony Brook Farm in Boston, to Ryan's ranch in Tennessee, this romantic comedy will sweep you away. Annie is actively pursued by a man full of confidence and godliness. She is still struggling with the pain of losing her husband and the fear of opening her heart up to another. As Annie learns to trust in God in a way that she has never trusted anyone, God heals her heart in a away that only He can do.

One

The person in the shadows took a few steps closer toward her. He was still on the outer edges of the light. Annie couldn't make out his features clearly, but she could feel him move. It was like a presence coming toward her. He was a big man, both broad and tall, yet he moved with the grace and swiftness of a dancer. His actions were bold and confident as if owned the dark hallway they were both in. A cold chill ran up Annie's spine, and she slowly turned to run.

"I heard you crying through the stage door." The voice was unexpectedly kind, and carried genuine concern with it. "I was wondering if there was anything I could do to help."

As Annie self-consciously backhanded the tears away from her eyes, she cautiously turned around to face the stranger again. He had moved fully into the light now, away from the cover of darkness. When her eyes rested upon his face, her jaw swung open in shock and a loud airy gasp escaped from her mouth.

"You don't need to be afraid of me," the man said gently, as if he were speaking to a frightened child.

All Annie could do was stare at him, openly and wide eyed, in a numb sort of trance, like a deer caught in a set of oncoming headlights. She couldn't have been more shocked if she had actually seen a ghost. She tried to concentrate on her breathing, and force herself to take slow, deep, even breathes. It wasn't working very well, and neither was her brain at the moment. She suddenly felt she had all the intelligence, confidence, and beauty of a slug. It was extremely unnerving.

The man standing in front of her was drop dead gorgeous. He looked like a Greek god come to life. He was very athletic looking and at least six feet tall. His tanned skin looked like an artist with incredible skill had sculpted it over his high cheekbones. His light brown hair had distinguished red high lights to it. It had been carefully styled and was cut shorter on the sides and left longer on the top. He wore a trendy stubble beard that a toothless smile now pierced.

Yet it wasn't his appearance that had Annie stalled in her tracks. The man standing before her, that she was inspecting so carefully, closely resembled a man she had buried six feet under two years earlier. The similarities were not only amazing, they were down right alarming. It left her mind boggled as she struggled with the confusion playing in her head. The sight of him did nothing less then chill her to the very core.

Annie forced herself to look into his eyes. Maybe the windows to his soul would provide some answers. He had deep blue gentle eyes. His steady eyes weren't afraid to look directly into hers. He had the type of eyes where you instantly felt that he could see down to your very heart and soul. The type of eyes, Annie thought as she examined the man closely, that not only searched for the truth, but also demanded it.

Annie knew she was staring at him. She was studying his face longer then she should have, but she couldn't seem to help it. The more she looked into those deep blue eyes, the more she was simply drawn in. Like a strong current pulling her, she had little choice as to where she would go.

Annie immediately noticed the change in his eyes. They had gone from being easy going and friendly, to dark and intense. The eyes that she had been lost in a moment ago now studied her with intentional, calculated appraisal. His pleasant smile had vanished and been replaced by a firm, hard, unwelcoming expression.

Annie knew this change in him had been because of her actions toward him. He didn't

understand why she was staring at him. He probably thought she was like an untamed teenager,
gawking at his appearance. She felt annoyed with
herself for letting him get under her skin like this.
She knew she would have to act, and act quickly.

Annie thrust her hand socially toward the man.
In a nervous voice, that sounded faster then a
speeding train, she rattled off her name. "Hi. I'm
Annie Smith. I'm so sorry to have disturbed you.
This is incredibly embarrassing for me."

The man stared at her hand for a second before
grabbing it and shaking it almost mechanically.
Confusion was spread plainly across his face. It
was clear that he did not know what to make of this
lady before him. "I'm Ryan Jones," he mumbled
out. He looked at her with a puzzled expression,
making no secret of the fact that he was trying his
best to figure her out.

The brief contact of their hands touching caused
an emotional explosion inside of Annie. She felt an
instant and unexplainable attraction to this man
that left her feeling bewildered and confused. Her
system had gone completely haywire at his very
touch, and pure instinct told her to run.

Annie closed her eyes for a moment. "How
weird is this?" she thought shaking her head, as if
it would somehow make her wake up from the
nightmare she had been thrown into. She had run

into the very man she was trying to avoid, and escape from. When she had seen Ryan up on stage, the resemblance he had to her late husband was so close that it was unbelievable. She left the auditorium to get away from him, and now she found herself standing face to face with him. It was too much. The more she thought of it, the more off balanced she felt.

She exhaled loudly and opened her eyes. Annie immediately became aware of the fact that Ryan Jones was watching her. No, she thought nervously, not just watching, but really dissecting her. A wave of extreme nervousness washed over Annie so hard it almost wiped her out. As she looked up into Ryan's eyes, she could now see that she was not the only one that had been affected. The simple touch of their hands had made him unsteady as well. Very interesting.

As he looked back at her, directly into her eyes, his casual look turned into a stare. For a moment, time stood still. The secret was out in the open. A man and woman, on the brink of something that neither anticipated, but both understood. More then simple attraction, need, or desire, there was a connection of their hearts that neither one of them could deny.

Annie's eyes narrowed in disgust. Never before in her life had a stranger affected her so quickly and so deeply. It frightened her and annoyed her. She took a step backwards to put some much-needed space between them. Life had been tough lately. She felt over worked, over tired, over stressed, and over weight. Everything was just over, Annie thought angrily, including this stupid meeting.

As she turned to go, the tone in Ryan's voice made her stop and turn around. The sudden gentleness in his voice took her off guard. His tone was full of genuine concern, and she couldn't shake it.

"Do you want to talk about what's bothering you? Sometimes it helps to talk about things."

"Yeah, and sometimes it doesn't," Annie replied firmly. She wanted to let him know that her problems were not about to be thrown on the table for discussion - especially with him. As soon as he had walked into the light, he no longer became a stranger to her. He was Ryan Jones, the contemporary Christian singer that she and her daughter had come to hear. He was a major heartthrob of teen girls and woman alike. She didn't want to fall for his charming personality, which he was famous for, or fall for his sparkling blue eyes, captivating smile, strong jaw, broad shoulders, inner strength... The list was getting longer by the moment, and regardless of what was on the menu, Annie wasn't hungry. She didn't want to have a apart of him.

Annie was not more then a few steps away when his voice cut through the uncomfortable gulf of silence like an alarm. "Hey!" he said in an excited tone, snapping his fingers together victoriously, "I knew I recognized your face! Now I've placed you!"

Annie regretfully turned back toward him. She was feeling more panicked, and if possible, more embarrassed. When was this nightmare going to end?"

"You're that Christian writer." Ryan's voice held all the enthusiasm of a contestant winning a TV game show. "You're the one who writes all those romantic mysteries."

Annie stiffened and smiled awkwardly. "Guilty," she responded quietly, wishing she could crawl under a rock and hide. To be caught crying in front of a famous celebrity, and then gawking at him like a heart sick teenager was well beyond her normal level of humiliation. She wanted to die from the embarrassment of it all.

"My wife…" Ryan went on, apparently unaware of Annie uneasiness, "was a big fan of yours. She read all your books- several times each!"

He ended with a flashy, yet completely charming smile that caught Annie off guard and made her go weak in the knees. As she struggled with the emotional tidal wave washing over her, Ryan's story came rushing back to her.

Ryan Jones's wife, Kay, had died about two years ago from breast cancer. Annie looked at Ryan compassionately, "I am so sorry about your wife."

Ryan nodded seriously. "Yeah, it's been a tough road." He paused for a minute and looked away. When he looked back, there was no mistaking the struggle of emotions that Annie saw in his eyes. "But, "he said trying to gain back his enthusiasm, "she loved your books. Your characters were like friends to her."

Annie smiled warmly and began to relax. "I'm glad. God uses all kinds of avenues to reach our hearts."

"That's true," Ryan agreed thoughtfully. "Hey, are you planning a sequel to *Red River*?"

Annie's eyebrows flew upwards as she looked at him in surprise.

Ryan shoved his hands into his jean pockets and chewed on the corner of his lip a moment before answering. Looking at her a bit shyly, he scuffed his toe against the cement floor. "I'm kind of a fan too. You see, when Kay became so sick that she couldn't read, I spent hours reading to her from the Bible and your books."

What an incredible guy, Annie thought as she studied him in a new light. Not just any guy would read romance novels to his wife, whether she was sick or not. "I'm not sure about a sequel," Annie replied slowly. She was beginning to feel like she was talking to an old friend.

"Well," Ryan's blue eyes had a sparkle of excitement to them as he spoke, "I think you should. It was a great story-definitely one that you should develop and expand further."

Annie smiled and laughed lightly. "Spoken from the mouth of another writer." She knew that Ryan wrote most of his songs, even the more romantic ones that he always dedicated to his wife.

"So," he asked in a caring tone that touched Annie's heart, "are you going to tell me what you were crying about?" As he shoved his hands back into his jean pockets, he tilted his head slightly and studied her with careful consideration. Once again Annie got the feeling that his eyes were searching her soul. It was unnerving to say the least.

"My husband was a big fan of yours," Annie blurted out quicker then she intended. "Your music just brings back a lot of memories."

Ryan nodded sympathetically. "It's hard. I know." As he put a gentle hand on Annie's shoulder, she looked up at him and felt as though she were going to weep from all the understanding she saw in his eyes. They had been through similar circumstances and understood each other's pain from losing a spouse. No words were necessary. They both understood the depth of suffering the valley had brought. The price they both had paid cost them dearly. Like soldiers returning from war, they carried scars with them, yet theirs were scars of the heart.

"Here we are talking about my wife's death, when I forgot that your husband recently passed away. How long has it been?"

Annie tired to smile courageously, but failed miserably. "Almost two years," she replied softly, avoiding his tender gaze by making it a mission to intently study her shoe. "You look so much like my husband, that when you came out on stage, I kind of lost it."

When Annie gained the courage, she glanced back up to meet Ryan's eyes. To her dismay, she found them lit with humor. He was leaning casually against the wall, with his arms folded easily across his broad chest. His eyebrows were raised slightly, as if to clearly challenge the truth of her story. As Annie took a closer look, she saw that he looked like a man trying very hard to restrain his laughter. To Annie's irritation, she realized she was not only going to be the target for his laughter, she was the reason for it as well. Alarm slammed through Annie as it suddenly hit her that Ryan thought she was coming unto him. Her faced flamed instantly, and she backed away from him clumsily.

"Wait a minute," she blurted out nervously, "let me show you." After rummaging through her wallet for a moment, she proudly produced a picture of her late husband and quickly thrust it at Ryan. It was her justification. Her proof.

The amusement drained from his face immediately, as if someone had pulled the plug. His mouth dropped opened slightly, and Annie felt an immense amount of satisfaction knowing that Ryan now understood that he and her late husband's appearance were remarkably similar. They looked so much alike they could easily pass not only as brothers, but also as twins.

"This is incredible." Ryan's voice was soft and full of awe. "I mean," he stuttered, "to have someone look so much like me, and not be me, is a really strange thing."

Annie smiled victoriously. "And you thought I was coming unto you!" She couldn't contain that laughter that slipped through her smiling lips. "That's not the type of girl that I am Ryan. I realize," Annie stated in a sarcastic tone laced with humor, "that most woman are drawn to you like kids are to candy. Let's get one thing straight. I am not applying to be the flavor of the month, or this week's trophy."

The toothy grin on Ryan's face sent a clear message to Annie that he was too amused by her words to be the least bit offended by them. He was actually enjoying her rebuke, and it annoyed her, knocking all the humor out of her. "It wasn't meant as a compliment," Annie grumbled. Ryan's smile actually grew wider and he let out a loud laugh. He was looking at her so audaciously, like he had every right in the world to tease her. It only fueled her already growing anger.

As Annie lifted her hand to grab her picture back, Ryan saw it coming and raised the picture higher, so it was just out of her reach. She stared at the picture that was dangling over her head, and felt her temper quickly rise. "What is with you? Give it back now. I'm not playing games here."

Once again, Annie got the feeling that her actions were only amusing him. It was extremely annoying, to say the very least. As she was about to give him another earful, he spoke in a more serious tone that caught her attention.

"Listen, can I hang unto this until after the concert? I'd like to discuss the picture with you, but I don't have time right now."

Annie's Irish temper began to boil. Now she was quite sure this world famous heartthrob of a Christian singer was coming unto her. "Mr. Jones," her voice was full of warning, "as hard as it may be for you to believe, I have no interest in discussing anything with you. Just give me my picture back now."

Again, to Annie's annoyance, he simply laughed. "Now you think that I'm coming unto you!" Ryan laughed again. His eyes were lit up mischievously, and it only mad her madder. "I'd just like to have a cup of coffee Annie, and talk about this." He flipped the picture slightly in his hand.

Annie stared at the picture a moment before answering him. "Mr. Jones," her voice was firm, "I am not interested in going on a date…"

Ryan interrupted her. Smiling impishly, he said in a flirting voice, "Annie, did you just think that I asked you out on a date?"

Annie rolled her eyes as she could feel her face heating up to a toasty shade of neon red. "How many times can I embarrass myself in front of this man," Annie yelled at herself silently. Once again, she got that all too familiar feeling of wanting to crawl under a rock. "Please," she begged in a help-less voice, "could I just have my picture back?"

Just then the side door to the stage opened, and an older man stuck his head out. "Five minutes to concert time, Ryan."

Ryan nodded to the man while sticking Annie's picture in his shirt pocket. "Listen," he said quick-ly in a serious voice, "meet me at the bus after the concert. I'll tell Gil, my driver, to expect you. I don't have time to explain right now, but we really do need to talk." Ryan then made a dash for the stage door, and was gone.

Annie stared at the stage door numbly. Her confused mind was still trying to make sense of what had just happened. Ryan Jones had taken her favorite picture of her late husband and disappeared with it. Heatedly, Annie paced the darkened hallway as she thought of what to do next.

"And now," Annie spoke angrily out loud, "the only way I can get my picture back is to meet this Romeo at his touring bus!" Annie threw a hand furiously in the air. "How incredibly arrogant! What nerve! How completely presumptuous of him."

Annie paced the hallway for another ten minutes, with steam pouring out her ears. As she thought about how much she disliked Ryan Jones and his music, a thought popped into her head. "Amy and Jimmy..." Annie stopped pacing for a moment. Her daughter Amy, and her friend from school, Jimmy, had dragged Annie to this concert. Eighteen-year-old Amy kept telling her that she was working too hard and needed to take a break.

"Fine," Annie said determinedly, "they will help me get my picture back and protect me from this Romeo."

As Annie marched back into the Rhode Island concert hall, to find Amy and Jimmy, she promised herself that she would throw away all of Ryan

Jones's tapes and CD's as soon as she got home. She never wanted to listen to his music again. If he thought this little prank of his was meant to entice her, he had failed big time. Mr. Jones had messed with the wrong woman, and he was just about to find out what a tornado her Irish temper could create if given the right opportunity. Annie paused for a second. This was definitely an opportunity, and she already felt her temper rising to the occasion.

Sawyer's Crossing

A New England Novel

Sharon Snow Sirois

Available
at
Your Local Bookstore

Sawyer's Crossing

Kelly Douglas returns to her hometown to fulfill a lifelong dream of becoming a police officer. Sawyer's Crossing is a small, picturesque Vermont town known for its many covered bridges and quaint New England styled shops.

It is in this close-knit community that Kelly quietly begins to conduct her own investigation into the unsolved murders of her parents. As the shocking truth of the investigation unfolds, Kelly finds herself not only the target of the man she's hunting, but the bait for him as well!

Mark Mitchell, the new police chief of Sawyer's Crossing, is a man that Kelly both admires and fears. He is a determined, dedicated, attractive young man, intent on not only capturing the murderer, but capturing Kelly's heart forever.

As Kelly and Mark unite to solve this crime, painful scars from the past threaten their investigation and their promising future together. Will they allow God to heal the past and replace their pain and fear with His perfect peace and love?

Prologue

"Daddy, please...," the little girl begged earnestly, as she excitedly jumped up and down.

Her father watched her lovingly, as her long, blonde ponytails gently bounced in the air. The young father smiled tenderly at his six-year-old daughter. He knew that he would have a hard time denying that little angel-face much of anything. She was so sweet and innocent and almost always cheerful. The little energetic bundle reminded him so much of his wife that his heart couldn't help but overflow with love for the child.

"OK, Kelly," the young father kissed her quickly on her rosy cheek," you go and hide, and I'll come and look for you in a few minutes."

Kelly ran out of the small kitchen, squealing with delight, as her parents sat at the old wooden table, watching her go. "Jerry," Rachel said as she rubbed her pregnant tummy, "Kelly is the only six-year-old that I know of that thinks the game is called 'Cops and Robbers,' and not 'Hide and Go Seek.'"

Jerry let out a loud, hearty laugh that filled the air. "Rach, don't blame me! Kelly made up the game herself! Actually," he grew serious, and arched his dark eyebrows upward, "you should really take pity on me."

"Pity?" Rachel eyed him suspiciously.

"Yeah, Rach," he said in a sad voice, "because I'm a cop, Kelly always makes me play a cop. I never get to hide and be the robber. Kelly always insists that I find her!"

They both laughed. Jerry's case wasn't very convincing. The love and pride that he felt toward his little girl was spread like a banner across his glowing face. Jerry sighed contentedly. At twenty-eight years old, he felt like he was the luckiest man on earth. He was married to his high school sweetheart, had a wonderful daughter and a baby on the way, and he was doing a job that he loved to do. Life couldn't be better for him. He reached across the table, and tenderly squeezed his wife's hand. "I'm living a dream, Rach. I love you."

As Kelly lay quietly under the old, sagging couch, she was able to watch her parents clearly. She smiled as she saw her daddy take her mommy's hand. Then, she looked curiously at her mommy's belly. She wondered for the hundredth time if God was going to give her a baby brother or a baby sister. She honestly didn't care what she got; she just wanted another kid to play with.

As Kelly intently watched her parents, she saw the back door suddenly fly open. A man dressed in black clothes came running over to her daddy. Kelly immediately felt frightened by the man's huge size. He was the biggest man that she had ever seen. Kelly's small body lay motionless and rigid, as she listened to angry words tumble from the big man's mouth. Kelly decided instantly that he must be a bad, bad man. Nobody ever talked to her daddy that way. Everyone loved daddy … except for this mean, giant, man.

Then Kelly saw it. Flickering in the kitchen light, she could clearly see that the bad man had a gun. Kelly was squeezing her doll so tightly, that her fingers hurt. She wanted to yell, or cry, but she couldn't. She felt too afraid.

"You took away the best years of my life, Douglas!" The big man yelled bitterly at Kelly's daddy. "And now, Douglas, it's time for me to take away the best years of your life!"

"No, Pitman!" Jerry Douglas yelled right before the shot went off. Kelly watched in horror as Pitman shot her daddy three times in the head.

Then Pitman spun around quickly and shot Kelly's mommy twice. As the big man walked slowly out of the kitchen, he said in an evil voice that shook Kelly's small body, "Too bad you married a cop, Lady. I don't believe in leaving any witnesses around."

Kelly rubbed her large blue eyes in disbelief. She watched, waiting for her daddy and mommy to get up off the floor, but they didn't. They didn't even move. Finally, in a small, trembling voice, she squeaked out, "Daddy? Mommy?"

Her parents' only response was silence. A paralyzing terror gripped Kelly as her daddy's words came racing back to her. "Never play with guns, Kelly. Guns can kill." Right then and there, in that sickening moment, Kelly knew the honest truth. Guns had killed...both her mommy and daddy. As she stared wide-eyed at the gruesome sight in front of her, a wave of cold, hard fear washed over her. What if the bad man came back? What if he came back and found her!

Quickly Kelly slid out from under the couch. She ran to her parents' bedroom, and dialed 911, just as her daddy had taught her to do. When a man answered the call, Kelly dropped the phone in fear. Maybe it was the bad man. She felt too frightened and confused to know for sure. She ran to her room and slid under her bed.

Still clutching her doll, she cried until she heard the sirens. They stopped outside the small Cape, and almost instantly voices filled the tiny kitchen. So many voices...Kelly thought listening carefully.

She didn't recognize any of them, until one called her name out.

"Where's Kelly?" the voice asked sounding panicked. "Jerry and Rachel are here, but where's Kelly?"

A moment later, he was shouting her name. "KELLY! KELLY!" She heard the man running through the house. Even as he called to her, she felt completely helpless to move.

A moment later, the man was lying on his stomach, on the floor, and looking at her, under her bed. He gently took her by the arms, and slowly pulled her out. "Oh, Sweetheart... Sweetheart," he said in a choked-up voice, as he held Kelly tightly. For the first time since the shooting, Kelly began to feel a little safe.

"Kelly," the man's voice was quiet and tender, "it's Uncle Baily. It's OK now, Honey. I won't let anyone hurt you."

The fifty-year-old police chief of Sawyer's Crossing, whom Kelly affectionately called Uncle Baily, rocked the little girl gently. He picked her up, into his strong protective arms, and carried her out the front door to his squad car. "Kelly," Baily said in a voice full of concern, as he slowly began to drive down the road, "I'm going to take you to your Grandma Wheeler's. OK?" Kelly numbly nodded. Her small body was shaking violently.

"Bad man...," Kelly said in a quiet, but angry voice. "He was a bad, bad man."

Uncle Baily pulled the squad car to the side of the road. "Kelly," he asked in an alarmed voice, "did you see this happen? Did you actually see the bad man?"

Kelly simply nodded. Her voice was suddenly gone.

"Sweetheart," Baily said in a troubled voice, full of warning, "don't tell anyone that you saw that bad man. Whoever did this to your daddy and mommy...he's...," Baily shuddered in fear, "he's sick! If the papers or TV get word around that you've seen him...that bad man may come after you! You're the only one who has seen him, Kelly. You're the only witness that can identify him. Oh, dear God...," Baily prayed in a frightened voice. "Kelly, whatever you do, Honey, don't tell anyone that you've seen him. "Sweetheart," he protectively covered his large hand over her small one, "right here, right now...you must take an oath of silence. Promise Uncle Baily that you'll never tell anyone, and," he said in a determined voice, "Uncle Baily will promise you that he will personally find that killer. I will find him, Kelly...," he looked at the small child intently, "I will find the man that killed your mommy and daddy if it's the last thing that I do on this earth."

One

$\mathcal{A}$s Kelly entered Baily's office at the Sawyer's Crossing police station, she felt as though she were stepping back in time, to her childhood. Baily's office had been a second home for Kelly, complete with special desk drawers that held toys and candy for her. As she scanned the small, crowded office quickly, eyeing the floor-to-ceiling bookcases, and the plants that filled every inch of window space, Kelly began to feel overwhelmed at all the wonderful memories she had in this room. From all kinds of fast-food kid's meals, to endless games of checkers, Baily and Kelly had shared many a special moment and conversation in this very room. As Kelly bent down to pat Amos, Baily's old Golden Retriever, she smiled lovingly at the round, jolly man. Immediately after the death of her parents, Baily had actively stepped into her life as a loving father-figure. Even though Kelly had been brought up officially by her Grandma Wheeler, Baily had made a point to see her or talk to her every day.

Baily and his wife Mel, having no children of their own, welcomed Kelly into their hearts and lives with open arms. They shared birthdays and holidays together, family outings and daily adventures. When Kelly was a teenager and expressed interest in wearing a badge, like he did and her father had, Baily enthusiastically encouraged the girl, knowing that she would be a natural for the job.

As Kelly stood before Baily, at twenty-five, fresh out of college and the Vermont Police Academy, Baily smiled at her proudly. "Well, young lady," he waved her over to a chair in front of his desk, "now that you're an official officer here at Sawyer's Crossing, tell me how your first week went?"

Kelly's big blue eyes lit up with excitement, as she slowly tucked some strands of blonde hair behind her ear. "Oh, Uncle Baily," Kelly said in a sincere voice, straight from the heart, "I love my job. I love helping the people here at Sawyer. I feel it's a way that I can really make a difference in my corner of the world."

Baily smiled understandingly at Kelly. At five-eight, the thin, bubbly blonde with the milky white complexion and rosy pink cheeks was not only a knock out on the outside, but on the inside as well. Kelly had a heart of gold, with the confidence and enthusiasm to make a great difference in their small, rural community.

"Well, Kelly," Baily stated proudly, "I'm not the least bit surprised. I knew you'd be a great addition to the force."

Kelly smiled back at the old chief, and in a teasing, spunky tone said, "Uncle Baily, I think you're just the slightest bit prejudiced toward me...but, thanks for the compliment anyway."

An unusual sober expression dropped across Baily's round, wrinkled face. "Well, hang onto the compliment Dear," Baily said in a heavy voice, because I'm afraid that you're not going to like what I have to say next."

Kelly stiffened and leaned forward in her chair. She looked intently at Baily, her eyes already narrowing in the anticipation of bad news.

"Kelly," Baily addressed her in a serious voice, filled with regret, "you know this time has been coming for a while...I promised to hang on until you made the force."

Kelly interrupted him, with an urgent, almost accusing tone. "You're not retiring, Baily!" She hastily pushed herself up from the chair. "I've only been here for a week! You can't do it," Kelly objected adamantly.

Baily smiled tenderly at Kelly. "Kelly, the Doc says I have to. My heart isn't as strong as it should be..."

"Your heart's fine, Baily!" Kelly shot back angrily. "First you hit me with retiring...then this heart thing! I don't want to hear it!" Kelly was really angry now, and her blue eyes were shooting electric sparks at the old chief.

"You're not even old enough to retire!" Kelly said in a last ditch effort to strengthen her case.

Baily let out a loud, jolly laugh, that to Kelly's annoyance bubbled freely through the small room. "Sweetheart,...I'm pushing seventy."

Kelly swung around, and stared at Baily in shock.

"You've grown up, Sweetheart...," he smiled at her lovingly, "and," he raised his bushy gray eyebrows, "I've grown old."

Kelly squinted her eyes at Baily in a disapproving way. "You're not old, Baily!" She stated emphatically. Then Kelly let out a loud sigh, filled with turbulent emotions. "Oh, Baily," Kelly whispered with a heavy heart, as she wiped some tears from her eyes, "no one can ever replace you."

A moment later, alarm covered Kelly's face. "You didn't already hire some jerk to replace you, did you?" Kelly asked urgently, suddenly feeling as though someone had thrown her out of a plane without a parachute. Her small, safe world was abruptly and unexpectedly crumbling to pieces before her eyes.

Baily nodded slightly, and waved a hand at someone behind Kelly. "Officer Kelly Douglas," Baily said in a formal voice, "I'd like you to meet the next Chief of Police at Sawyer's Crossing... Capt. Mark Mitchell."

Kelly spun around in shock, and stared openly at a tall, blonde-haired man, casually walking into Baily's office. He had a friendly face that seemed to break easily into a smile, and an honest and genuine sense about himself. Yet, as Kelly continued to eye him disapprovingly, she thought the young man looked more like a model in a cop's uniform, than a real cop.

As he warmly extended his hand to her, he said in a sincere voice, "It's a pleasure to meet you, Officer Douglas. I'm Mark Mitchell."

Kelly couldn't seem to help it. Her next words just flew out of her mouth. "You seem awfully young, Capt. Mitchell," she said in a disapproving tone.

Baily laughed loudly. "I told you, Mark. Kelly is going to be the toughest one to win over."

Kelly gave Baily a hard, cold scowl that most others would have fainted from, but the old chief just laughed harder. After all the years he had known Kelly, he had come to predict her reactions accurately, and anticipate her directness.

Mark's eyes had narrowed slightly, but in a voice that still maintained its friendly tone, he said directly to Kelly, "I guess I do seem young, Officer Douglas, but I'll let my record speak for itself."

An awkward silence was broken by the ever optimistic Baily. "Mark's only thirty-five, but he's done more in his years as a cop down in D.C., than most people have done in a lifetime."

"D.C.!" Kelly practically yelled at Baily. "You hired a city-slicker to replace you, Baily! You know you should have hired a Green Mountain Boy from Vermont."

Mark's body had grown rigid now, and his stance was definitely defensive. He still wore a partial smile plastered to his face, but one look into his stormy blue eyes gave Kelly an accurate indication of the anger mounting inside of him. "I grew up in Bennington, Vermont, Officer Douglas," Mark replied in a firm voice that commanded respect. "I still consider myself a 'Green Mountain Boy.'" He was sounding more like a police chief with every passing moment, and the feeling made Kelly increasingly uneasy.

Kelly looked at Mitchell in surprise. She knew she should apologize to him, but she just couldn't bring herself to do it. "I need to go," Kelly turned her angry eyes back to Baily. "Gram is expecting me."

With that said, Kelly turned and headed out the door, without so much as even glancing in Mitchell's direction. Kelly had known Mitchell for all of ten minutes, and she already hated him. No one could ever replace Baily, Kelly thought angrily. Especially, she thought grumbling under her breath, not a thirty-five year old city-slicker.

Two

The very next morning, Baily introduced Mark Mitchell to the entire Sawyer's Crossing police department. Baily's pride in the new chief was evident, and everyone seemed genuinely pleased except for Kelly.

"Wipe that smile off your face, Rand," Kelly whispered angrily to her partner, "unless you want me clobbering you in the nose!"

Rand Thompson was a friendly, low-key type of guy, even though his imposing linebacker size implied otherwise. He smiled sadly at Kelly, realizing the transition would be harder on her than anyone else on the force. "Sorry, Kel...," his tone was compassionate, "I know this is rough on you."

"Yeah, well," Kelly couldn't hide her sarcasm, "everyone else seems to be welcoming 'Golden Boy' with open arms."

Just then, Mitchell turned around and looked directly at her. By the amused expression on his face, Kelly was quite sure that he had heard her comment. As Mitchell walked slowly toward her, he looked like a man trying hard to contain his laughter. "Douglas," he said in a firm voice, that was lightly laced with humor, "I'd like to see you in my office immediately."

Kelly should have been concerned, and slightly intimidated, but she wasn't. "Your office?" Kelly demanded in a questioning voice.

Mitchell turned around to face her with an expression that held just a trace of anger. "Yes, Officer Douglas," he stated in a commanding tone. "My office. Now."

Kelly followed him, with her temper growing hotter each step of the way. This man is completely impossible, she thought as she bored raging eyes into his back. Even though he appeared friendly on the outside, she was sure he was a power-hungry, commanding jerk on the inside.

As Kelly followed Mitchell into Baily's old office, she stopped abruptly in her tracks. As she surveyed the once cherished room, it appeared as though it had been struck by a tornado. Boxes and boxes of Mitchell's things were piled everywhere, and not one single item of Baily's remained, including the plants. Kelly's eyes dropped to the worn area on the carpet that Amos was always curled up on, and she felt oddly strange inside not seeing the old dog there. How could things change so fast, Kelly thought shaking her head. Literally, overnight, her world had changed, and she knew this change would not be for the better.

Mitchell eyed Kelly understandingly as she continued to take in the changes. "Baily moved his things out last night," his voice had grown quiet and thoughtful. Kelly stared at Mitchell with such a surprised expression, that she couldn't even nod. The full impact of Baily's retirement was just slapping her in the face now. Reality can be so cruel, Kelly thought bitterly. As she continued to stare at the new chief, her eyes narrowed furiously. It was all Mitchell's fault, Kelly decided quickly. She felt as though Chief Mark Mitchell was invading a private place in her life. This old, dusty room was so special to her heart that she felt as though Mitchell was intruding by just being in here. As Mitchell started to speak, Kelly threw her hands on her hips defiantly.

"Douglas," he addressed her in a firm, but quiet tone, "I realize that this is going to be harder on you than most. But," his tone was growing steadily firmer, "I am your new boss, and I expect to be treated with respect. You don't have to like me," he said in a tone that was clearly indifferent, "but we need to get along well enough to work together professionally."

As Kelly studied the fair-haired model, it suddenly struck her that Mitchell didn't like her any more than she liked him. Everything was changing at this moment. Mitchell was clearly laying the cards on the table for her. He was her new boss. He was the man who could make her life miserable in Sawyer's Crossing. And, Kelly thought dismally, he was the man who could ultimately fire her.

Kelly immediately tried to mask her dislike of the man. "I'm sure we can work together professionally, Chief Mitchell." Kelly knew her voice sounding strained, and it only made her comment less convincing. Mitchell studied her through intense eyes, searching her face for the truth. Then, in a steady voice, he said honestly, "I certainly hope so, Officer Douglas."

Kelly watched as Mitchell dropped down into Baily's old seat, behind Baily's old desk. The sight of him behind Baily's desk angered her all over again.

Kelly watched Mitchell in a rigid, determined way as he gazed at a paper in his hand. "I'm going to be meeting with all the staff one on one, to get to know them." Mitchell stated in a casual tone. "And," he looked up from his paper and smiling charmingly at Kelly, "you get to be my first victim."

Kelly was fairly sure that he meant victim in a friendly way, but it still made her stiffen and pull the walls in tighter around her.

"Tell me, Officer Douglas," Mitchell said in a curious voice, "why it is that someone who graduates first in their class in college and first in their class at the Academy would want to work in a small town like Sawyer's Crossing?"

OK, Kelly thought, narrowing her heated eyes at him, "victim" is a very accurate word. Her sinking opinion of Chief Mitchell just plummeted. "Why wouldn't I want to work in Sawyer's Crossing?" Kelly replied defiantly, purposely answering his question with one of her own.

Mitchell paused, and studied her for a moment. The intense scrutiny of his gaze made Kelly want to look away, but she forced herself to meet his stare, and hold his eyes with all the courage she could find. After what seemed like an eternity, Mitchell spoke in a firm, but quiet voice, that held just an edge of hardness to it. "You're a tough case, Douglas. I just wanted to know what drew you to a small place like Sawyer? Most kids your age would be running off for the bright lights of the big city."

His statement only piqued Kelly's temper, and for a moment she lost her head. "You mean like you did!" she blurted out in a voice that dripped with resentment. Instantly, she covered her mouth with her hand. She couldn't believe that she had actually said that to his face, and judging from the hard expression on Mitchell's face, neither could he.

He's going to fire me before this interview is over, Kelly thought panicking. "I'm sorry, Sir," Kelly said quickly, in a nervous, almost desperate tone. "That was completely uncalled for. I was out of line."

Mitchell's jaw tightened, and he continued to dissect Kelly through heated, examining eyes of his own. She felt herself practically melting under his inspection.

Kelly continued hastily, "I wanted to work in Sawyer's Crossing, Sir, because this is my home. This is where I grew up. I love this place."

Her honest answer seemed to take some of the wind out of Mitchell's anger. "Do you still have family here?" he asked intently, not taking his investigating eyes off her for an instant.

Kelly turned her eyes away from his probing, penetrating stare. "A grandmother," Kelly replied, in a quiet voice.

"No parents or siblings?" he persisted.

Kelly tensed. There was no way that she was going to explain about her parents to Mitchell. That was too personal an issue, and, as far as she was concerned, completely none of his business. "No, Sir," Kelly replied evenly. "Gram and I are the only ones left in Sawyer."

He nodded, but seemed surprised. "That must be difficult for you. I'm sure you must miss your family.

Kelly was completely taken off guard momentarily by Mitchell's sincere, compassionate voice. Something in his voice had hit a nerve deep down. As she looked in Mitchell's eyes, to identify the emotion, whatever she had heard was no longer there. Quickly, Kelly reverted back to her shell. "Yes, Sir," she replied in a masked voice, "I miss my family."

After a few more questions, Mitchell dismissed Kelly. There was something evasive about the young cop, and Mitchell couldn't decide if it was due to Baily's retirement or something more. He made a note to keep an eye on Kelly Douglas, both professionally and personally. There was something about the young officer that drew him to her, and yet, at the same time, something that almost haunted him. There was something deep in her eyes, but he couldn't put his finger on it. Time will tell, Mitchell finally concluded. Reluctantly, he knew that time was the only thing on his side as far as Kelly Douglas was concerned.

Three

"I'm supposed to be driving!" Kelly said in an irritated voice to her friend and partner Rand Thompson.

The big man just laughed lightly. "Yeah, I know, Kelly...," he answered in an amused tone, "but with you behind the wheel as angry as you are, I feel like I'd be committing suicide!" Rand let out another laugh, as Kelly poked him in the side.

Kelly tried to act angry, but she couldn't. Rand's observation was correct. She was steamed. "You know," Kelly said defensively, "I was in a good mood until Mitchell laid his pep talk on us this morning."

Rand laughed loudly this time. "Why do you let Mitchell get under your skin, Kel? You need to take things more in stride. Beside...," Rand looked over at her seriously, "he was right."

Kelly turned quickly in her seat and eyed her partner intently. "You really agree with him?" Kelly said in disgust.

Rand glanced at her and smiled. "Yes, Kel, I do. I think the speeding in Sawyer's Crossing has got to stop. This is a tourist town, and people speeding around it make it dangerous."

Rand paused, and then laughed loudly. "You know," he teased, "if Mitchell really wanted to control the speeding problem, all he'd have to do is take away one license."

"Oh yeah, Wise Guy...," Kelly asked in her best intimidating voice, "and just whose license are you talking about?"

"Yours!" Rand shot back seriously. "You drive that Celica of yours like it's a rocket." Kelly smiled, and smacked his arm playfully. "Really, Kel," he looked at his partner with concern, "you need to slow down, and be careful. No one downtown is going to fix your speeding tickets for you anymore since Baily's retired. You're on your own now."

Kelly sighed heavily. "That is a major problem for me, Rand. I hate driving slow!"

"Yeah, well, practice, Kelly," Rand's voice was void of any sympathy. "Mitchell already seems at odds enough with you. You don't need to go looking for trouble."

"Thanks for your concern, Rand," Kelly replied in a sarcastic tone.

Rand just laughed.

"You know," Kelly said in a kinder voice, "you're lucky that you're married to my best friend.

If you weren't, I would have clobbered you a long time ago."

"I know!" Rand laughed loudly. "Becca is my insurance policy!"

Kelly's day ended without so much as a single battle with Mitchell. As she climbed the front porch to Gram's house, she decided that her best plan against the "Golden Boy" would be to avoid him at all costs. Any time she had to talk to him, it only seemed to put her at further odds with the new chief.

Wearily, Kelly skipped the kitchen and headed straight to bed. It was late and she knew that Gram would be in bed already, but even so, as she always had done, she checked in on the old woman. Gram was the sunshine in her life. The old woman loved the Lord so much that it seemed to ripple into every area of her life. Kelly was glad that the old woman had God, but she did not share the same belief. At five years old, Kelly had given her heart to the Lord. At six, after her parents had died, she had taken it back. She still felt that if God was really so good, he would have never allowed her parents to be murdered.

The only reason she went to church on Sundays, was to please Gram. She loved Gram dearly and would never do anything to hurt the woman. If that meant suffering through church once a week, she would. It was a small price to pay for all that Gram had done for her.

That night, the dreams came back in full force. Kelly was six again, and hiding under the couch with her doll. For the millionth time, she watched in horror as the bad man shot her parents. It was all so real that Kelly found herself screaming at the top of her lungs hysterically.

The next thing that she knew was that Gram was at her side holding her and rocking her gently. "Kelly! Kelly!" The old woman said lovingly. "Wake up, Sweetheart. You're having a bad dream."

As Kelly opened her eyes and looked up in the direction of the comforting, reassuring voice, she instantly recognized her grandmother's face. Gram smiled warmly at her, and just continued talking to her frightened granddaughter tenderly. "Precious child, you are all right. You are safe, Kelly, and no one's going to hurt you."

As usual, Kelly buried her face against Gram's chest, and wept uncontrollably. "Oh, Gram," Kelly asked in a painful voice, between her heart wrenching sobs, "when will it ever stop? When will the nightmares end?"

"Oh, sweet, sweet Kelly...," Gram voice was tearful, "you have suffered so much for someone so young. I wish I could stop them, honey. I wish I could take all your pain away."

They held each other for several more minutes, and then Gram returned to her room. Kelly sat up in bed wiping her damp face. "How long," she whispered fearfully to the darkness in her room, "how long will I have to live through that horrible day? Is it ever going to go away?"

As Gram lay in bed, quietly sobbing and praying, she begged her Heavenly Father for help. "Oh, dear Father, the girl has suffered so much...and these awful nightmares...almost every night for nineteen years...it's too much, dear Lord. It's too much for anyone to go through. Please make them stop, dear God. For Kelly's sake, make them stop. Please give Kelly her life back. She's so young, and she's such a tortured soul. Help her Father. Help her turn to You. I know You're the only one who can give the child back her life."

Four

$\mathcal{T}$he next morning arrived too early for Kelly, and she inadvertently slept through her alarm clock. The nightmares had ruined almost every night's sleep she had, and getting up proved to be almost unbearable.

After Gram had gently awakened her, she quickly showered and dressed in her dark navy uniform. One good thing about wearing a uniform, Kelly thought, smiling at her police uniform, was that she never had to worry about what outfit she would wear to work.

As Kelly jumped into her red Toyota Celica, she munched on a piece of toast that Gram had shoved into her hand as she ran out the door. As she drove her little sports car down Tim's Path, she was suddenly reminded of Rand's warning to slow down. Kelly glanced at the clock on her dashboard and pressed the accelerator a little harder. "If I slow down, Rand," she said in a heated voice, "I'm going to be late for work!"

When Kelly rounded a corner, she instantly saw the black and white cruiser. It was partially hidden behind the pine trees, and its lights went on even before she had passed it. Angrily she jammed the accelerator harder. "Not today, Micky!" she said in a determined voice.

As Kelly glanced in her rearview mirror, Micky was still behind her, but at a distance. As Micky closed the gap between them, Kelly could clearly see two patrolmen in the cruiser. Her mouth dropped open, as her eyes did a quick double take. Her heart almost stopped beating as she noticed the tall, blonde officer next to Micky. It undoubtedly was her worst nightmare...Chief Mitchell.

"I'm dead!" Kelly completely panicked. "I am so dead that it isn't even funny."

Kelly knew that Mitchell would have her badge for outrunning a cruiser, so immediately her mind went to plan B. "I need to outrun him and lose him," she said in a determined, hopeful voice.

Kelly jammed the accelerator harder, bringing her speed up to 60 in a 35 M.P.H. zone. She downshifted the Celica, and slowed only momentarily, as she skillfully maneuvered a sharp right turn through the industrial section of Sawyer. She weaved her way in and out of buildings, with her tires screeching loudly, and then finally down a long brick alley that led directly to the police station. With no cruiser in sight, Kelly literally ran into the station and flew down the stairs into the morning briefing room.